A Philological Essay Concerning the Pygmies of the Ancients

Edward Tyson

Contents

A PHILOLOGICAL ESSAY CONCERNING THE PYGMIES OF THE ANCIENTS

BY

Edward Tyson

TO MY DEAR MOTHER

PREFATORY NOTE

It is only necessary for me to state here, what I have mentioned in the Introduction, that my account of the habits of the Pigmy races of legend and myth makes no pretence of being in any sense a complete or exhaustive account of the literature of this subject. I have contented myself with bringing forward such tales as seemed of value for the purpose of establishing the points upon which I desire to lay emphasis.

I have elsewhere expressed my obligations to M. De Quatrefage's book on Pigmies, obligations which will be at once recognised by those familiar with that monograph. To his observations I have endeavoured to add such other published facts as I have been able to gather in relation to these peoples.

I have to thank Professors Sir William Turner, Haddon, Schlegel, Brinton, and Topinard for their kindness in supplying me with information in response to my inquiries on several points.

Finally, I have to acknowledge my indebtedness to Professor Alexander Macalister, President of the Anthropological Institute, and to Mr. E. Sidney Hartland, for their kindness in reading through, the former the first two sections, and the latter the last two sections of the Introduction, and for the valuable suggestions which both have made. These gentlemen have laid me under obligations which I can acknowledge, but cannot repay.

BERTRAM C. A. WINDLE.
MASON COLLEGE,
BIRMINGHAM, 1894.

INTRODUCTION

I.

Edward Tyson, the author of the Essay with which this book is concerned, was, on the authority of Monk's Roll of the Royal College of Physicians, born, according to some accounts, at Bristol, according to others, at Clevedon, co. Somerset, but was descended from a family which had long settled in Cumberland. He was educated at Magdalene Hall, Oxford, as a member of which he proceeded Bachelor of Arts on the 8th of February 1670, and Master of Arts on the 4th of November 1673. His degree of Doctor of Medicine he took at Cambridge in 1678 as a member of Corpus Christi College. Dr. Tyson was admitted a candidate of the College of Physicians on the 30th of September 1680, and a Fellow in April 1683. He was Censor of the College in 1694, and held the appointments of Physician to the Hospitals of Bridewell and Bethlem, and of Anatomical Reader at Surgeons' Hall. He was a Fellow of the Royal Society, and contributed several papers to the "Philosophical Transactions." Besides a number of anatomical works, he published in 1699 "A Philosophical Essay concerning the Rhymes of the Ancients," and in the same year the work by which his name is still known, in which the Philological Essay which is here reprinted finds a place. Tyson died on the 1st of August 1708, in the fifty-eighth year of his age, and is buried at St. Dionis Backchurch. He was the original of the Carus not very flatteringly described in Garth's "Dispensary."

The title-page of the work above alluded to runs as follows:--

Orang-Outang, sive Homo Sylvestris:

OR, THE ANATOMY OF A PYGMIE

Compared with that of a ***Monkey***, an ***Ape***, and a ***Man***.

To which is added, A PHILOLOGICAL ESSAY Concerning the *Pygmies*, the *Cynocephali*, the *Satyrs*, and *Sphinges* of the ANCIENTS.

Wherein it will appear that they are all either *APES* or *MONKEYS*, and not *MEN*, as formerly pretended.

By *EDWARD TYSON* M.D.

Fellow of the Colledge of Physicians, and the Royal Society: Physician to the Hospital of *Bethlem*, and Reader of Anatomy at *Chirurgeons-Hall*.

LONDON:

Printed for *Thomas Bennet* at the *Half-Moon in St. Paul's* Church-yard; and *Daniel Brown* at the *Black Swan* and *Bible* without *Temple-Bar* and are to be had of Mr. *Hunt* at the *Repository* in *Gresham-Colledge*. M DC XCIX.

It bears the authority of the Royal Society:--

17 deg. *Die Maij*, 1699.

Imprimatur Liber cui Titulus, *Orang-Outang, sive Homo Sylvestris,* &c. Authore *Edvardo Tyson*, M.D. R.S.S.

JOHN HOSKINS, *V.P.R.S*.

The Pygmy described in this work was, as a matter of fact, a chimpanzee, and its skeleton is at this present moment in the Natural History Museum at South Kensington. Tyson's granddaughter married a Dr. Allardyce, who was a physician of good standing in Cheltenham. The "Pygmie" formed a somewhat remarkable item of her dowry. Her husband presented it to the Cheltenham Museum, where it was fortunately carefully preserved until, quite recently, it was transferred to its present position.

At the conclusion of the purely scientific part of the work the author added four Philological Essays, as will have appeared from his title-page. The first of these is both the longest and the most interesting, and has alone been selected for republication in this volume.

This is not the place to deal with the scientific merit of the main body of Tyson's work, but it may at least be said that it was the first attempt which had been made to deal with the anatomy of any of the anthropoid apes, and that its execution shows very conspicuous ability on the part of its author.

Tyson, however, was not satisfied with the honour of being the author of an important morphological work; he desired to round off his subject by considering its bearing upon the, to him, wild and fabulous tales concerning pigmy races. The various allusions to these races met with in the pages of the older writers, and discussed in his, were to him what fairy tales are to us. Like modern folk-lorists, he wished to explain, even to euhemerise them, and bring them into line with the science of his day. Hence the "Philological Essay" with which this book is concerned. There are no pigmy races, he says; "the most diligent enquiries of late into all the parts of the inhabited world could never discover any such puny diminutive race of mankind." But there are tales about them, "fables and wonderful and merry relations, that are transmitted down to us concerning them," which surely require explanation. That explanation he found in his theory that all the accounts of pigmy tribes were based upon the mistakes of travellers who had taken apes for men. Nor was he without followers in his opinion; amongst whom here need only be mentioned Buffon, who in his *Histoire des Oiseaux* explains the Homeric tale much as Tyson had done. The discoveries, however, of this century have, as all know, re-established in their essential details the accounts of the older writers, and in doing so have demolished the theories of Tyson and Buffon. We now know, not merely that there are pigmy races in existence, but that the area which they occupy is an extensive one, and in the remote past has without doubt been more extensive still. Moreover, certain of these races have been, at least tentatively, identified with the pigmy tribes of Pliny, Herodotus, Aristotle, and other writers. It will be well, before considering this question, and before entering into any consideration of the legends and myths which may possibly be associated with dwarf races, to sketch briefly their distribution throughout the continents of the globe. It is necessary to keep clearly in view the upper limit which can justly be assigned to dwarfishness, and with this object it may be advisable to commence with a statement as to the average heights reached by various representative peoples. According to Topinard, the races of the world may be classified, in respect to their stature, in the following manner:--

Tall	5 ft. 8 in. and upwards.
Above the average	5 ft. 6 in. to 5 ft. 8 in.
Below the average	5 ft. 4 in. to 5 ft. 6 in.
Short	Below 5 ft. 4 in.

Thus amongst ordinary peoples there is no very striking difference of height, so far as the average is concerned. It would, however, be a great mistake to suppose that all races reaching a lower average height than five feet four inches are, in any accurate sense of the word, to be looked upon as pigmies. We have to descend to a considerably lower figure before that appellation can be correctly employed. The stature must fall considerably below five feet before we can speak of the race as one of dwarfs or pigmies. Anthropometrical authorities have not as yet agreed upon any upward limit for such a class, but for our present purposes it may be convenient to say that any race in which the average male stature does not exceed four feet nine inches--that is, the average height of a boy of about twelve years of age--may fairly be described as pigmy. It is most important to bear this matter of inches in mind in connection with points which will have to be considered in a later section.

Pigmy races still exist in considerable numbers in Asia and the adjacent islands, and as it was in that continent that, so far as our present knowledge goes, they had in former days their greatest extension, and, if De Quatrefages be correct, their place of origin, it will be well to deal first with the tribes of that quarter of the globe. "The Negrito" (*i.e.*, pigmy black) "type," says the authority whom I have just quoted, and to whom I shall have to be still further indebted,[A] "was first placed in South Asia, which it without doubt occupied alone during an indeterminate period. It is thence that its diverse representatives have radiated, and, some going east, some west, have given rise to the black populations of Melanesia and Africa. In particular, India and Indo-China first belonged to the blacks. Invasions and infiltrations of different yellow or white races have split up these Negrito populations, which formerly occupied a continuous area, and mixing with them, have profoundly altered them. The present condition of things is the final result of strifes and mixtures, the most ancient of which may be referred back to prehistoric times." The invasions above mentioned having in the past driven many of the races from the mainland to the islands, and those which remained on the continent having undergone greater modification by crossing with taller and alien races, we may expect to find the purest Negritos amongst the tribes inhabiting the various archipelagoes situated south and east of the mainland. Amongst these, the Mincopies of the Andaman Islands offer a convenient starting-point. The knowledge which we possess of these little blacks is extensive, thanks to the labours in particular of Mr. Man[B] and

Dr. Dobson,[C] which may be found in the Journal of the Anthropological Institute, and summarised in De Quatrefages' work. The average stature of the males of this race is four feet six inches, the height of a boy of ten years of age. Like children, the head is relatively large in comparison with the stature, since it is contained seven times therein, instead of seven and a half times, as is the rule amongst most average-sized peoples. Whilst speaking of the head, it may be well to mention that these Negritos, and in greater or less measure other Negritos and Negrillos (*i.e.*, pigmy blacks, Asiatic or African), differ in this part of the body in a most important respect from the ordinary African negro. Like him, they are black, often intensely so: like him, too, they have woolly hair arranged in tufts, but, unlike him, they have round (brachycephalic) heads instead of long (dolichocephalic); and the purer the race, the more marked is this distinction. The Mincopie has a singularly short life; for though he attains puberty at much the same age as ourselves, the twenty-second year brings him to middle life, and the fiftieth, if reached, is a period of extreme senility. Pure in race, ancient in history, and carefully studied, this race deserves some further attention here than can be extended to others with which I have to deal. The moral side of the Mincopies seems to be highly developed; the modesty of the young girls is most strict; monogamy is the rule, and--

"Their list of forbidden degrees
An extensive morality shows,"

since even the marriage of cousins-german is considered highly immoral. "Men and women," says Man, "are models of constancy." They believe in a Supreme Deity, respecting whom they say, that "although He resembles fire, He is invisible; that He was never born, and is immortal; that He created the world and all animate and inanimate objects, save only the powers of evil. During the day He knows everything, even the thoughts of the mind; He is angry when certain sins are committed, and full of pity for the unfortunate and miserable, whom He sometimes condescends to assist. He judges souls after death, and pronounces on each a sentence which sends them to paradise or condemns them to a kind of purgatory. The hope of escaping the torments of this latter place influences their conduct. Puluga, this Deity, inhabits a house of stone; when it rains, He descends upon the earth in search of food; during the dry weather He is asleep." Besides this Deity, they believe in numerous evil spirits, the chief of whom is the Demon of the Woods. These spirits have created themselves, and have existed *ab immemorabili*. The sun, which is a female, and the moon, her husband, are secondary deities.

[A: The quotations from this author are taken from his work *Les Pygmees*. Paris, J.B. Bailliere et Fils, 1887.]

[B: *Jour. Anthrop. Inst.*, vii.]

[C: *Ibid.*, iv.]

South of the Andaman Islands are the Nicobars, the aborigines of which, the Shom Pen,[A] now inhabit the mountains, where, like so many of their brethren, they have been driven by the Malays. They are of small, but not pigmy stature (five feet two inches), a fact which may be due to crossing.

[A: Man, *Jour. Anthrop. Inst.*, xviii. p. 354.]

Following the Negritos east amongst the islands, we find in Luzon the Aetas or Inagtas, a group of which is known in Mindanao as Manamouas. The Aetas live side by side with the Tagals, who are of Malay origin. They were called Negritos del Monte by the Spaniards who first colonised these islands. Their average stature, according to Wallace, ranges from four feet six inches to four feet eight inches. In New Guinea, the Karons, a similar race, occupy a chain of mountains parallel to the north coast of the great north-western peninsula. At Port Moresby, in the same island, the Koiari appear to represent the most south-easterly group; but my friend Professor Haddon, who has investigated this district, tells me that he finds traces of a former existence of Negritos at Torres Straits and in North Queensland, as shown by the shape of the skulls of the inhabitants of these regions.

The Malay Peninsula contains in Perak hill tribes called "savages" by the Sakays. These tribes have not been seen by Europeans, but are stated to be pigmy in stature, troglodytic, and still in the Stone Age. Farther south are the Semangs of Kedah, with an average stature of four feet ten inches, and the Jakuns of Singapore, rising to five feet. The Annamites admit that they are not autochthonous, a distinction which they confer upon the Mois, of whom little is known, but whose existence and pigmy Negrito characteristics are considered by De Quatrefages as established.

China no longer, so far as we know, contains any representatives of this type, but Professor Lacouperie[A] has recently shown that they formerly existed in that part of Asia. According to the annals of the Bamboo Books, "In the twenty-ninth year of the Emperor Yao, in spring, the chief of the Tsiao-Yao, or dark pigmies, came to court and offered as tribute feathers from the Mot." The Professor continues, "As shown by this entry, we begin with the semi-historic times as recorded in the 'Annals of the Bamboo Books,' and the date about 2048 B.C. The so-called feathers were simply some sort of marine plant or seaweed with which the immigrant Chinese, still an inland people, were yet unacquainted. The Mot water or river, says the Shan-hai-king, or canonical book of hills and seas, was situated in the south-east of the Tai-shan in Shan-tung. This gives a clue to the localisation of the pigmies, and this localisation agrees with the positive knowledge we possess of the small area which the Chinese dominion covered at this time. Thus the Negritos were part of the native population of China when, in the twenty-third century B.C., the civilised Bak tribes came into the land." In Japan we have also evidence of their existence. This country, now inhabited by the Niphonians, or Japanese, as we have come to call them, was previously the home of the Ainu, a white, hairy under-sized race, possibly, even probably, emigrants from Europe, and now gradually dying out in Yezo and the Kurile Islands. Prior to the Ainu was a Negrito race, whose connection with the former is a matter of much dispute, whose remains in the shape of pit-dwellings, stone arrow-heads, pottery, and other implements still exist, and will be found fully described by Mr. Savage Landor in a recent most interesting work.[B] In the Shan-hai-king, as Professor Schlegel[C] points out, their country is spoken of as the Siao-jin-Kouo, or land of little men, in distinction, be it noted, to the Peh-min-Kouo, or land of white people, identified by him with the Ainu. These little men are spoken of by the Ainu as Koro-puk-guru, *i.e.*, according to Milne, men occupying excavations, or pit-dwellers. According to Chamberlain, the name means dwellers under burdocks, and is associated with the following legend. Before the time of the Ainu, Yezo was inhabited by a race of dwarfs, said by some to be two to three feet, by others only one inch in height. When an enemy approached, they hid themselves under the great leaves of the burdock (**koro**), for which reason they are called Koro-puk-guru, i.e., the men under the burdocks. When they were exterminated by the wooden clubs of the Ainu, they raised their eyes to heaven, and, weeping, cried aloud to the gods, "Why were we made so small?" It should be said that Professor Schlegel and Mr. Savage Landor both seem to prefer the former etymology.

[A: Babylonian and Oriental Record, vol. v.]

[B: Alone with the Hairy Ainu.]

[C: ***Problemes Geographiques. Les Peuples Etrangers chez les Historiens Chinois***. Extrait du T'oung-pao, vol. *iv*. No. 4. Leide, E.J. Brill.]

Passing to the north-west of the Andamans, we find in India a problem of considerable difficulty. That there were at one period numerous Negrito tribes inhabiting that part of Asia is indubitable; that some of them persist to this day in a state of approximate purity is no less true, but the influence of crossing has here been most potent. Races of lighter hue and taller stature have invaded the territory of the Negritos, to a certain extent intermarried with them, and thus have originated the various Dravidian tribes. These tribes, therefore, afford us a valuable clue as to the position occupied in former days by their ancestors, the Negritos.

In some of the early Indian legends, De Quatrefages thinks that he finds traces of these prehistoric connections between the indigenous Negrito tribes and their invaders. The account of the services rendered to Rama by Hanuman and his monkey-people may, he thinks, easily be explained by supposing the latter to be a Negrito tribe. Another tale points to unions of a closer nature between the alien races. Bhimasena, after having conquered and slain Hidimba, at first resisted the solicitations of the sister of this monster, who, having become enamoured of him, presented herself under the guise of a lovely woman. But at the wish of his elder brother, Youdhichshira, the king of justice, and with the consent of his mother, he yielded, and passed some time in the dwelling of this Negrito or Dravidian Armida.

It will now be necessary to consider some of these races more or less crossed with alien blood.

In the centre of India, amongst the Vindyah Mountains, live the Djangals or Bandra-Lokhs, the latter name signifying man-monkey, and thus associating itself with the tale of Rama, above alluded to. Like most of the Dravidian tribes, they live in great misery, and show every sign of their condition in their attenuated figures. One of this tribe measured by Rousselet was five feet in height. It may here be remarked that the stature of the Dravidian races exceeds that of the purer Negritos, a fact due, no doubt, to the influence of crossing. Farther south, in the Nilgherry Hills, and in the neighbourhood of the Todas and Badagas, dwell the Kurumbas.

and Irulas (children of darkness). Both are weak and dwarfish, the latter especially so. They inhabit, says Walhouse,[A] the most secluded, densely wooded fastnesses of the mountain slopes. They are by popular tradition connected with the aboriginal builders of the rude stone monuments of the district, though, according to the above-mentioned authority, without any claim to such distinction. They, however, worship at these cromlechs from time to time, and are associated with them in another interesting manner. "The Kurumbas of Nulli," says Walhouse, "one of the wildest Nilgherry declivities, come up annually to worship at one of the dolmens on the table-land above, in which they say one of their old gods resides. Though they are regarded with fear and hatred as sorcerers by the agricultural B[)a]d[)a]gas of the table-land, one of them must, nevertheless, at sowing-time be called to guide the first plough for two or three yards, and go through a mystic pantomime of propitiation to the earth deity, without which the crop would certainly fail. When so summoned, the Kurumba must pass the night by the dolmens alone, and I have seen one who had been called from his present dwelling for the morning ceremony, sitting after dark on the capstone of a dolmen, with heels and hams drawn together and chin on knees, looking like some huge ghostly fowl perched on the mysterious stone." Mr. Gomme has drawn attention to this and other similar customs in the interesting remarks which he makes upon the influence of conquered non-Aryan races upon their Aryan subduers.[B]

[A: *Jour. Anthrop. Inst.*, vii. 21.]

[B: Ethnology and Folk-Lore, p. 46; The Village Community, p. 105.]

Farther south, in Ceylon, the Veddahs live, whom Bailey[A] considers to be identical with the hill-tribes of the mainland, though, if this be true, some at least must have undergone a large amount of crossing, judging from the wavy nature of their hair. The author just quoted says, "The tallest Veddah I ever saw, a man so towering above his fellows that, till I measured him, I believed him to be not merely comparatively a tall man, was only five feet three inches in height. The shortest man I have measured was four feet one inch. I should say that of males the ordinary height is from four feet six inches to five feet one inch, and of females from four feet four inches to four feet eight inches."

[A: *Trans. Ethn. Soc.*, ii. 278.]

In the east the Santals inhabit the basin of the Ganges, and in the west the Jats belong to the Punjab, and especially to the district of the Indus. The Kols inhabit the delta of the Indus and the neighbourhood of Gujerat, and stretch almost across Central India into Behar and the eastern extremities of the Vindhya Mountains. Other Dravidian tribes are the Oraons, Jouangs, Buihers, and Gounds. All these races have a stature of about five feet, and, though much crossed, present more or less marked Negrito characteristics. Passing farther west, the Brahouis of Beluchistan, a Dravidian race, who regard themselves as the aboriginal inhabitants, live side by side with the Belutchis. Finally, in this direction, there seem to have been near Lake Zerrah, in Persia, Negrito tribes who are probably aboriginal, and may have formed the historic black guard of the ancient kings of Susiana.

An examination of the present localisation of these remnants of the Negrito inhabitants shows how they have been split up, amalgamated with, or driven to the islands by the conquering invaders. An example of what has taken place may be found in the case of Borneo, where Negritos still exist in the centre of the island. The Dyaks chase them like wild beasts, and shoot down the children, who take refuge in the trees. This will not seem in the least surprising to those who have studied the history of the relation between autochthonous races and their invaders. It is the same story that has been told of the Anglo-Saxon race in its dealings with aborigines in America, and notably, in our case, in Tasmania.

Turning from Asia to a continent more closely associated, at least in popular estimation, with pigmy races, we find in Africa several races of dwarf men, of great antiquity and surpassing interest. The discoveries of Stanley, Schweinfurth, Miani, and others have now placed at our disposal very complete information respecting the pigmies of the central part of the continent, with whom it will, therefore, be convenient to make a commencement. These pigmies appear to be divided into two tribes, which, though similar in stature, and alike distinguished by the characteristic of attaching themselves to some larger race of natives, yet present considerable points of difference, so much so as to cause Mr. Stanley to say that they are as unlike as a Scandinavian is to a Turk. "Scattered," says the same authority,[A] "among the Balesse, between Ipoto and Mount Pisgah, and inhabiting the land between the Ngaiyu and Ituri rivers, a region equal in area to about two-thirds of Scotland, are the Wambutti, variously called Batwa, Akka, and Bazungu. These people are under-sized nomads, dwarfs or pigmies, who live in the uncleared virgin forest, and support themselves on game, which they are very expert in catching. They vary in height from three feet to four feet six inches. A full-grown adult may weigh ninety pounds. They plant their village camps three miles around a tribe of agricultural aborigines, the majority of whom are fine stalwart people. They use poisoned arrows, with which they kill elephants, and they capture other kinds of game by the use of traps."

[A: In Darkest Africa, vol. ii. p. 92.]

The two groups are respectively called Batwa and Wambutti. The former inhabit the northern parts of the above-mentioned district, the latter the southern. The former have longish heads, long narrow faces, and small reddish eyes set close together, whilst the latter have round faces and open foreheads, gazelle-like eyes, set far apart, and rich yellow ivory complexion. Their bodies are covered with stiffish grey short hair. Two further quotations from the same source may be given to convey an idea to those ignorant of the original work, if such there be, of the appearances of these dwarfs. Speaking of the queen of a tribe of pigmies, Stanley says,[A] "She was brought in to see me, with three rings of polished iron around her neck, the ends of which were coiled like a watch-spring. Three iron rings were suspended to each ear. She is of a light-brown complexion with broad round face, large eyes, and small but full lips. She had a quiet modest demeanour, though her dress was but a narrow fork clout of bark cloth. Her height is about four feet four inches, and her age may be nineteen or twenty. I notice when her arms are held against the light a whity-brown fell on them. Her skin has not that silky smoothness of touch common to the Zanzibaris, but altogether she is a very pleasing little creature." To this female portrait may be subjoined one of a male aged probably twenty-one years and four feet in height.[B] "His colour was coppery, the fell over the body was almost furry, being nearly half an inch long, and his hands were very delicate. On his head he wore a bonnet of a priestly form, decorated with a bunch of parrot feathers, and a broad strip of bark covered his nakedness."

[A: In Darkest Africa, vol. i. p. 345.]

[B: Ibid., ii. 40.]

Jephson states[A] that he found continual traces of them from 270 30' E. long., a few miles above the Equator, up to the edge of the great forest, five days' march from Lake Albert. He also says that they are a hardy daring race, always ready for war, and are much feared by their neighbours. As soon as a party of dwarfs makes its appearance near a village, the chief hastens to propitiate them by presents of corn and such vegetables as he possesses. They never exceed four feet one inch in height, he informs us, and adds a characteristic which has not been mentioned by Stanley, one, too, which is very remarkable when it is remembered how scanty is the facial hair of the Negros and Negritos--the men have often very long beards. The southern parts of the continent are occupied by the Bushmen, who are vigorous and agile, of a stature ranging from four feet six inches to four feet nine inches, and sufficiently well known to permit me to pass over them without further description. The smallest woman of this race who has been measured was only three feet three inches in height, and Barrow examined one, who was the mother of several children, with a stature of three feet eight inches. The Akoas of the Gaboon district were a race of pigmies who, now apparently extinct, formerly dwelt on the north of the Nazareth River. A male of this tribe was photographed and measured by the French Admiral Fleuriot de l'Angle. His age was about forty and his stature four feet six inches.

[A: Emm Pasha, p. 367, et seq.]

Flower[A] says that "another tribe, the M'Boulous, inhabiting the coast north of the Gaboon River, have been described by M. Marche as probably the primitive race of the country. They live in little villages, keeping entirely to themselves, though surrounded by the larger Negro tribes, M'Pongos and Bakalais, who are encroaching upon them so closely that their numbers are rapidly diminishing. In 1860 they were not more than 3000; in 1879 they were much less numerous. They are of an earthy-brown colour, and rarely exceed five feet three inches in height. Another group living between the Gaboon and the Congo, in Ashangoland, a male of which measured four feet six inches, has been described by Du Chaillu."

In Loango there is a tribe called Babonko, which was described by Battell in 1625, in the work entitled "Purchas his Pilgrimes," in the following terms:--"To the north-east of Mani-Kesock are a kind of little people called Matimbas; which are no bigger than boyes of twelve yeares old, but very thicke, and live only upon flesh, which they kill in the woods with their bows and darts. They pay tribute to Mani-Kesock, and bring all their elephants' teeth and tayles to him. They will not enter into any of the Maramba's houses, nor will suffer any one to come where they dwell. And if by chance any Maramba or people of Longo pass where they dwell, they will forsake that place and go to another. The women carry bows and arrows as well as the men. And one of these will walk in the woods alone and kill the Pongos with their poysoned arrows." It is somewhat surprising that Tyson, who gives in his essay (p. 80) the account of the same people published at a later date (1686) by Dapper, should have missed his fellow-countryman's narrative. The existence of this tribe has been established by a German expedition, one of the members of which, Dr. Falkenstein, photographed and measured an adult male whose stature was four feet six inches.

Krapf[A] states that in the south of Schoa, in a part of Abyssinia as yet unworked, the Dokos live, who are not taller than four feet. According to his account, they are of a dark olive colour, with thick prominent lips, flat noses, small eyes, and long flowing hair. They have no dwellings, temples, holy trees, chiefs, or weapons, live on roots and fruit, and are ignorant of fire. Another group was described by Mollieu in 1818 as inhabiting Tenda-Maie, near the Rio Grande, but very little is known about them. In a work entitled "The Dwarfs of Mount Atlas," Halliburton[B] has brought forward a number of statements to prove that a tribe of dwarfs, named like those of Central Africa, Akkas, of a reddish complexion and with short woolly hair, live in the district adjoining Soos. These dwarfs have been alluded to by Harris and Doennenburg,[C] but Mr. Harold Crichton Browne,[D] who has explored neighbouring districts, is of opinion that there is no such tribe, and that the accounts of them have been based upon the examination of sporadic examples of dwarfishness met with in that as in other parts of the world.

[A: *Morgenblatt*, 1853 (quoted by Schaafhausen, *Arch. f. Anth.*, 1866, p. 166).]
[B: London, Nutt, 1891.]
[C: *Nature*, 1892, ii. 616.]
[A: *Nature*, 1892, i. 269.]

Finally, in Madagascar it is possible that there may be a dwarf race. Oliver[A] states that "the Vazimbas are supposed to have been the first occupants of Ankova. They are described by Rochon, under the name of Kunios, as a nation of dwarfs averaging three feet six inches in stature, of a lighter colour than the Negroes, with very long arms and woolly hair. As they were only described by natives of the coast, and have never been seen, it is natural to suppose that these peculiarities have been exaggerated; but it is stated that people of diminutive size still exist on the banks of a certain river to the south-west." There are many tumuli of rude work and made of rough stones throughout the country, which are supposed to be their tombs. In idolatrous days, says Mullens,[B] the Malagasy deified the Vazimba, and their so-called tombs were the most sacred objects in the country. In this account may be found further evidence in favour of Mr. Gomme's theory, to which attention has already been called.

[A: ***Anthrop. Memoirs***, iii. 1.]

[B: ***Jour. Anthrop. Inst.***, v. 181.]

In the great continent of America there does not appear to have ever been, so far as our present knowledge teaches, any pigmy race. Dr. Brinton, the distinguished American ethnologist, to whom I applied for information on this point, has been good enough to write to me that, in his opinion, there is no evidence of any pigmy race in America. The "little people" of the "stone graves" in Tennessee, often supposed to be such, were children, as the bones testify. The German explorer Hassler has alleged the existence of a pigmy race in Brazil, but testimony is wanting to support such allegation. There are two tribes of very short but not pigmy stature in America, the Yahgans of Tierra del Fuego and the Utes of Colorado, but both of these average over five feet.

Leaving aside for the moment the Lapps, to whom I shall return, there does not appear to have been at any time a really pigmy race in Europe, so far as any discoveries which have been made up to the present time show. Professor Topinard, whose authority upon this point cannot be gainsaid, informs me that the smallest race known to him in Central Europe is that of the pre-historic people of the Lozere, who were Neolithic troglodytes, and are represented probably at the present day by some of the peoples of South Italy and Sardinia. Their average stature was about five feet two inches. This closely corresponds with what is known of the stature of the Platycnemic race of Denbighshire, the Perthi-Chwareu. Busk[A] says of them that they were of low stature, the mean height, deduced from the lengths of the long bones, being little more than five feet. As both sexes are considered together in this description, it is fair to give the male a stature of about five feet two inches,[B] It also corresponds with the stature assigned by Pitt-Rivers to a tribe occupying the borders of Wiltshire and Dorsetshire during the Roman occupation, the average height of whose males and females was five feet two and a half inches and four feet ten and three-quarter inches respectively.

[A: ***Jour. Ethn. Soc.***, 1869-70, p. 455.]

[B: Since these pages were printed, Prof. Kollmann, of Basle, has described a group of Neolithic pigmies as having existed at Schaffhausen. The adult interments consisted of the remains of full-grown European types and of small-sized people. These two races were found interred side by side under precisely similar conditions, from which he concludes that they lived peaceably together, notwithstanding racial difference. Their stature (about three feet six inches) may be compared with that of the Veddahs in Ceylon. Prof. Kollmann believes that they were a distinct species of mankind.]

Dr. Rahon,[A] who has recently made a careful study of the bones of pre-historic and proto-historic races, with special reference to their stature, states that the skeletons attributed to the most ancient and to the Neolithic races are of a stature below the middle height, the average being a little over five feet three inches. The peoples who constructed the Megalithic remains of Roknia and of the Caucasus, were of a stature similar to our own. The diverse proto-historic populations, Gauls, Franks, Burgundians, and Merovingians, considered together, present a stature slightly superior to that of the French of the present day, but not so much so as the accounts of the historians would have led us to believe.

[A: ***Recherches sur les Ossements Humaines, Anciens et Prehistonques. Mem. de la Soc. d'Anthrop. de Paris***, Ser, ii. tom. iv. 403.]

It remains now to deal with two races whose physical characters are of considerable importance in connection with certain points which will be dealt with in subsequent pages, I mean the Lapps and the Innuit or Eskimo.

The Lapps, according to Karonzine,[A] one of their most recent describers, are divisible into two groups, Scandinavian and Russian, the former being purer than the latter race. The average male stature is five feet, a figure which corresponds closely with that obtained by Mantegazza and quoted by Topinard. The extremes obtained by this observer amongst men were, on the one hand, five feet eight inches, and on the other four feet four inches. As, however, in a matter of this kind we have to deal with averages and not with extremes, we must conclude that the Lapps, though a stunted race, are not pigmies, in the sense in which the word is scientifically employed.

[A: *L'Anthropologie*, ii. 80.]

The Innuit or Eskimo were called by the original Norse explorers "Skraeling-jar," or dwarfs, a name now converted by the Innuit into "karalit," which is the nearest approach that they are able to make phonetically to the former term. They are certainly, on the average, a people of less than middle stature, yet they can in no sense be described as Pigmies. Their mean height is five feet three inches. Nansen[A] says of them, "It is a common error amongst us in Europe to think of the Eskimo as a diminutive race. Though no doubt smaller than the Scandinavian peoples, they must be reckoned amongst the middle-sized races, and I even found amongst those of purest breeding men of nearly six feet in height."

[A: *Eskimo Life*, p. 20.]

II.

The **raison d'etre** of Tyson's essay was to explain away the accounts of the older writers relating to Pigmy races, on the ground that, as no such races existed, an explanation of some kind was necessary in order to account for so many and such detailed descriptions as were to be found in their works. Having now seen not merely that there are such things as Pigmy races, but that they have a wide distribution throughout the world, it may be well to consider to which of the existing or extinct races, the above-mentioned accounts may be supposed to have referred. In this task I am much aided in several instances by the labours of De Quatrefages, and as his book is easily accessible, it will be unnecessary for me to repeat the arguments in favour of his decisions which he has there given.

Starting with Asia, we have in the first place the statement of Pliny, that "immediately after the nation of the Prusians, in the mountains where it is said are pigmies, is found the Indus." These Pigmies may be identified with the Brahouis, now Dravidian, but still possessing the habit, attributed to them by Pliny, of changing their dwellings twice a year, in summer and winter, migrations rendered necessary by the search for food for their flocks. The same author's allusion to the "Spithamaei Pygmaei" of the mountains in the neighbourhood of the Ganges may apply to the Santals or some allied tribe, though Pliny's stature for them of two feet four inches is exaggeratedly diminutive, and he has confused them with Homer's Pigmies, who were, as will be seen, a totally different people.

Ctesias[A] tells us that "Middle India has black men, who are called Pygmies, using the same language as the other Indians; they are, however, very little; that the greatest do not exceed the height of two cubits, and the most part only of one cubit and a half. But they nourish the longest hair, hanging down unto the knees, and even below; moreover, they carry a beard more at length than any other men; but, what is more, after this promised beard is risen to them, they never after use any clothing, but send down, truly, the hairs from the back much below the knees, but draw the beard before down to the feet; afterward, when they have covered the whole body with hairs, they bind themselves, using those in the place of a vestment. They are, moreover, apes and deformed. Of these Pygmies, the king of the Indians has three thousand in his train; for they are very skilful archers." No doubt the actual stature has been much diminished in this account, and, as De Quatrefages suggests, the garment of long floating grasses which they may well have worn, may have been mistaken for hair; yet, in the description, he believes that he is able to recognise the ancestors of the Bandra-Lokh of the Vindhya Mountains. Ctesias' other statement, that "the king of India sends every fifth year fifty thousand swords, besides abundance of other weapons, to the nation of the Cynocephali," may refer to the same or some other tribe.

[A: The quotation is taken from Ritson, *Fairy Tales*, P. 4.]

De Quatrefages also thinks that an allusion to the ancestors of the Jats, who would then have been less altered by crossing than now, may be found in Herodotus' account of the army of Xerxes when he says, "The Eastern Ethiopians serve with the Indians. They resemble the other Ethiopians, from whom they only differ in language and hair. The Eastern Ethiopians have straight hair, while those of Lybia are more woolly than all other men."

Writing of isles in the neighbourhood of Java, Maundeville says,[A] "In another yle, ther ben litylle folk, as dwerghes; and thei ben to so meche as the Pygmeyes, and thei han no mouthe, but in stede of hire mouthe, thei han a lytylle round hole; and whan thei schulle eten or drynken, thei taken thorghe a pipe or a penne or suche a thing, and sowken it in, for thei han no tongue, and therefore thei speke not, but thei maken a maner of hissynge, as a Neddre dothe, and thei maken signes on to another, as monkes don, be the whiche every of hem undirstondethe the other."

[A: Ed. Halliwell, p. 205.]

Strip this statement of the characteristic Maundevillian touches with regard to the mouth and tongue, and it may refer to some of the insular races which exist or existed in the district of which he is treating.

A much fuller account[A] by the same author relates to Pigmies in the neighbourhood of a river, stated by a commentator[B] to be the Yangtze-Kiang, "a gret ryvere, that men clepen Dalay, and that is the grettest ryvere of fressche water that is in the world. For there, as it is most narow, it is more than 4 myle of brede. And thanne entren men azen in to the lond of the great Chane. That ryvere gothe thorge the lond of Pigmaus, where that the folk ben of lityllle stature, that ben but 3 span long, and thei ben right faire and gentylle, aftre here quantytees, bothe the men and the women. And thei maryen hem, whan thei ben half zere of age and getten children. And thei lyven not, but 6 zeer or 7 at the moste. And he that lyveth 8 zeer, men holden him there righte passynge old. Theise men ben the beste worcheres of gold, sylver, cotoun, sylk, and of alle such thinges, of ony other, that be in the world. And thei han often tymes werre with the briddes of the contree, that thei taken and eten. This litylle folk nouther labouren in londes ne in vynes. But thei han grete men amonges hem, of oure stature, that tylen the lond, and labouren amonges the vynes for hem. And of the men of oure stature, han thei als grete skorne and wondre, as we wolde have among us of Geauntes, zif thei weren amonges us. There is a gode cytee, amonges othere, where there is duellynge gret plentee of the lytylle folk, and is a gret cytee and a fair, and the men ben grete that duellen amonges hem; but whan thei getten ony children, thei ben als litylle as the Pygmeyes, and therefore thei ben alle, for the moste part, alle Pygmeyes, for the nature of the land is suche. The great Cane let kepe this cytee fulle wel, for it is his. And alle be it, that the Pygmeyes ben litylle, zit thei ben fulle resonable, aftre here age and connen bothen wytt and gode and malice now." This passage, as will be noted, incorporates the Homeric tale of the battles between the Pigmies and the Cranes, and is adorned with a representation of such an encounter. Whether Maundeville's dwarfs were the same as the Siao-Jin of the Shan-hai-King is a question difficult to decide; but, in any case, both these pigmy races of legend inhabited a part of what is now the Chinese Empire. The same Pigmies seem to be alluded to in the rubric of the Catalan map of the world in the National Library of Paris, the date of which is A.D. 1375. "Here (N.W. of Catayo-Cathay) grow little men who are but five palms in height, and though they be little, and not fit for weighty matters, yet they be brave and clever at weaving and keeping cattle." If such an explanation may be hazarded, we may perhaps go further and suppose that Paulus Jovius may have been alluding to the Koro-puk-guru, when, as Pomponius Mela tells us, he taught that there were Pigmies beyond Japan. In both these cases, however, it is well to remember that there is a river in Macedon as well as in Monmouth, and that it is hazardous to come to too definite a belief as to the exact location of the Pigmies of ancient writers.

[A: *Maundeville*, p. 211.]

[B: *Quart. Rev.*, 172, p. 431.]

The continent of Africa yielded its share of Pigmies to the same writers. The most celebrated of all are those alluded to by Aristotle in his classical passage, "They (the Cranes) come out of Scythia to the Lakes above Egypt whence the Nile flows. This is the place whereabouts the Pigmies dwell. For this is no fable but a truth. Both they and the horses, as 'tis said, are of a small kind. They are Troglodytes and live in caves."

Leaving aside the crane part of the tale, which it has been suggested may really have referred to ostriches, Aristotle's Pigmy race may, from their situation, be fairly identified with the Akkas described by Stanley and others. That this race is an exceedingly ancient one is proved by the fact that Marriette Bey has discovered on a tomb of the ancient Empire of Egypt a figure of a dwarf with the name Akka inscribed by it. This race is also supposed to have been that which, alluded to by Homer, has become confused with other dwarf tribes in different parts of the world.

> "So when inclement winters vex the plain
> With piercing frosts or thick-descending rain,
> To warmer seas the cranes embodied fly,
> With noise and order, through the midway sky;
> To Pigmy nations wounds and death they bring,
> And all the war descends upon the wing."

Attention may here be drawn to Tyson's quotation (p. 78) from Vossius as to the trade driven by the Pigmies in elephants' tusks, since, as we have seen, this corresponds with what we now know as to the habits of the Akkas.

The account which Herodotus gives of the expedition of the Nasamonians is well known. Five men, chosen by lot from amongst their fellows, crossed the desert of Lybia, and, having marched several days in deep sand, perceived trees growing in the midst of the plain. They approached and commenced to eat the fruit which they bore. Scarcely had they begun to taste it, when they were surprised by a great number of men of a stature much inferior to the middle height, who seized them and carried them off. They were eventually taken to a city, the inhabitants of which were black. Near this city ran a considerable river whose course was from west to east, and in which crocodiles were found. In his account of the Akkas, Mr. Stanley believed that he had discovered the representatives of the Pigmies mentioned in this history. Speaking of one of these, he says,[A] "Twenty-six centuries ago his ancestors captured the five young Nasamonian explorers, and made merry with them at their villages on the banks of the Niger." It may be correct to say that, at the period alluded to, the dwarf races of Africa were in more continuous occupancy of the land than is now the case, but such an identification as that just mentioned gives a false idea of the position of the Pigmies of Herodotus. De Quatrefages, after a most careful examination of the question in all its aspects, finds himself obliged to conclude, either that the Pigmy race seen by the Nasamonians still exists on the north of the Niger, which has been identified with the river alluded to by Herodotus, but has not, up to the present, been discovered; or that it has disappeared from those regions.

[A: *Op. supra cit.*, ii. 40.]

Pomponius Mela has also his account of African Pigmies. Beyond the Arabian Gulf, and at the bottom of an indentation of the Red Sea, he places the Panchaeans, also called Ophiophagi, on account of the fact that they fed upon serpents. More within the Arabian bay than the Panchaeans are the Pigmies, a minute race, which became exterminated in the wars which it was compelled to wage with the Cranes for the preservation of its fruits. The region indicated somewhat corresponds with that which is assigned to the Dokos by their describer. In this district, too, other dwarf races have been reported. The French writer whom I have so often cited says, "The tradition of Eastern African Pigmies has never been lost by the Arabs. At every period the geographers of this nation have placed their River of Pigmies much more to the south. It is in this region, a little to the north of the Equator, and towards the 32 deg. of east longitude, that the Rev. Fr. Leon des Avanchers has found the Wa-Berrikimos or Cincalles, whose stature is about four feet four inches. The information gathered by M. D'Abbadie places towards the 6 deg. of north latitude the Mallas or Maze-Malleas, with a stature of five feet. Everything indicates that there exist, at the south of the Galla country, different negro tribes of small stature. It seems difficult to me not to associate them with the Pigmies of Pomponius Mela. Only they have retreated farther south. Probably this change had already taken place at the time when the Roman geographer wrote; it is, therefore, comprehensible that he may have regarded them as having disappeared."

Tyson (p. 29) quotes the following passage from Photius:--"That Nonnosus sailing from Pharsa, when he came to the farthermost of the islands, a thing very strange to be heard of happened to him; for he lighted on some (animals) in shape and appearance like men, but little of stature, and of a black colour, and thick covered with hair all over their bodies. The women, who were of the same stature, followed the men. They were all naked, only the elder of them, both men and women, covered their privy parts with a small skin. They seemed not at all fierce or wild; they had a human voice, but their dialect was altogether unknown to everybody that lived about them, much more to those that were with Nonnosus. They lived upon sea-oysters and fish that were cast out of the sea upon the island. They had no courage for seeing our men; they were frighted, as we are at the sight of the greatest wild beast." It is not easy to identify this race with any existing tribe of Pigmies, but the hairiness of their bodies, and above all their method of clothing themselves, leave no doubt that in this account we have a genuine story of some group of small-statured blacks.

From the foregoing account it will be seen that it is possible with more or less accuracy and certainty to identify most of those races which, described by the older writers, had been rejected by their successors. Time has brought their revenge to Aristotle and Pliny by showing that they were right, where Tyson, and even Buffon, were wrong.

III.

The little people of story and legend have a much wider area of distribution than those of real life, and it is the object of this section to give some idea of their localities and dwellings. Imperfect as such an account must necessarily be, it will yet suffice I trust in some measure to show that, like the England of Arthurian times, all the world is "fulfilled of faery."

In dealing with this part of the subject, it would be possible, following the example of Keightley, to treat the little folk of each country separately. But a better idea of their nature, and certainly one which for my purpose will be more satisfactory, can, I think, be obtained by classifying them according to the nature of their habitations, and mentioning incidentally such other points concerning them as it may seem advisable to bring out.

1. In the first place, then, fairies are found dwelling in mounds of different kinds, or in the interior of hills. This form of habitation is so frequently met with in Scotch and Irish accounts of the fairies, that it will not be necessary for me to burden these pages with instances, especially since I shall have to allude to them in a further section in greater detail. Suffice it to say, that many instances of such an association in the former country will be found in the pages of Mr. MacRitchie's works, whilst as to the latter, I shall content myself by quoting Sir William Wilde's statement, that every green "rath" in that country is consecrated to the "good people." In England there are numerous instances of a similar kind. Gervase of Tilbury in the thirteenth century mentions such a spot in Gloucestershire: "There is in the county of Gloucester a forest abounding in boars, stags, and every species of game that England produces. In a grovy lawn of this forest there is a little mount, rising in a point to the height of a man." With this mount he associates the familiar story of the offering of refreshment to travellers by its unseen inhabitants. In

Warwickshire, the mound upon which Kenilworth Castle is built was formerly a fairy habitation.[A] Ritson[B] mentions that the "fairies frequented many parts of the Bishopric of Durham." There is a hillock or tumulus near Bishopton, and a large hill near Billingham, both of which used in former time to be "haunted by fairies." Even Ferry-hill, a well-known stage between Darlington and Durham, is evidently a corruption of "Fairy-hill." In Yorkshire a similar story attaches to the sepulchral barrow of Willey How,[C] and in Sussex to a green mound called the Mount in the parish of Pulborough.[D] The fairies formerly frequented Bussers Hill in St. Mary's Isle, one of the Scilly group.[E] The Bryn-yr-Ellyllon,[F] or Fairy-hill, near Mold, may be cited as a similar instance in Wales, which must again be referred to.

[A: *Testimony of Tradition*, p. 142.]

[B: *Op. cit.*, p. 56.]

[C: *Folk Lore*, ii. 115.]

[D: *Folk Lore Record*, i. 16 and 28.]

[E: *Ritson*, p. 62.]

[F: Dawkins, *Early Man in Britain*, p. 433.]

The pages of Keightley's work contain instances of hill-inhabiting fairies in Scandinavia, Denmark, the Isle of Rugen, Iceland, Germany, and Switzerland. It is not only in Europe, however, that this form of habitation is to be met with; we find it also in America. The Sioux have a curious superstition respecting a mound near the mouth of the Whitestone River, which they call the Mountain of Little People or Little Spirits; they believe that it is the abode of little devils in the human form, of about eighteen inches high and with remarkably large heads; they are armed with sharp arrows, in the use of which they are very skilful. These little spirits are always on the watch to kill those who should have the hardihood to approach their residence. The tradition is that many have suffered from their malice, and that, among others, three Maha Indians fell a sacrifice to them a few years since. This has inspired all the neighbouring nations, Sioux, Mahas, and Ottoes, with such terror, that no consideration could tempt them to visit the hill.[A]

[A: Lewis and Clarke, *Travels to the Source of the Missouri River.* Quoted in *Flint Chips*, p. 346. The tale is also given in *Folk Lore, Oriental and American* (Gibbings & Co.), p. 45.]

The mounds or hills inhabited by the fairies are, however, of very diverse kinds, as we discover when we attempt to analyse their actual nature. In some cases they are undoubtedly natural elevations. Speaking of the exploration of the Isle of Unst, Hunt[A] says that the term "Fairy Knowe" is applied alike to artificial and to natural mounds. "We visited," he states, "two 'Fairy Knowes' in the side of the hill near the turning of the road from Reay Wick to Safester, and found that these wonderful relics were merely natural formations. The workmen were soon convinced of this, and our digging had the effect of proving to them that the fairies had nothing to do with at least two of these hillocks." The same may surely be said of that favourite and important fairy haunt Tomnahurich, near Inverness, though Mr. MacRitchie seems to think that an investigation, were such possible, of its interior, might lead to a different explanation.

[A: ***Anthrop. Mems.***, ii. 294.]

In other cases, and these are of great importance in coming to a conclusion as to the origin of fairy tales, the mounds inhabited by the little people are of a sepulchral nature. This is the case in the instance of Willey How, which, when explored by Canon Greenwell, was found, in spite of its size and the enormous care evidently bestowed upon its construction, to be merely a cenotaph. A grave there was, sunk more than twelve feet deep in the chalk rock; but no corporeal tenant had ever occupied it.

This fact is still more clearly shown in the remarkable case mentioned by Professor Boyd Dawkins. A barrow called Bryn-yr-Ellyllon (Fairy-hill), near Mold, was said to be haunted by a ghost clad in golden armour which had been seen to enter it. The barrow was opened in the year 1832, and was found to contain the skeleton of a man wearing a golden corselet of Etruscan workmanship.

The same may be said respecting that famous fairy-hill in Ireland, the Brugh of the Boyne, though Mr. MacRitchie seems to regard it as having been a dwelling-place. Mr. Coffey in a most careful study appears to me to have finally settled the question.[A] He speaks of the remains as those of probably the most remarkable of the pre-Christian cemeteries of Ireland. Of the stone basins, whose nature Mr. MacRitchie regards as doubtful, he says, "There can be hardly any doubt but that they served the purpose of some rude form of sarcophagus, or of a receptacle for urns." Mr. Coffey quotes the account from the Leadhar na huidri respecting cemeteries, in which Brugh is mentioned as amongst the chief of those existing before the faith (i.e. before the introduction of Christianity). "The nobles of the Tuatha de Danann were used to bury at Brugh (i.e. the Dagda with his three sons; also Lugaidh, and Oe, and Ollam, and Ogma, and Etan the Poetess, and Corpre, the son of Etan), and Cremthain followed them, because his wife Nar was of the Tuatha Dea, and it was she solicited him that he should adopt Brugh as a burial-place for himself and his descendants, and this was the cause that they did not bury at Cruachan." Mr. Coffey also quotes O'Hartagain's poem, which seems to bear in Mr. MacRitchie's favour:--

"Behold the sidhe before your eyes:
It is manifest to you that it is a king's mansion,
Which was built by the firm Dagda;
It was a wonder, a court, a wonderful hill."

[A: *Tumuli at New Grange. Trans. Roy. Irish Academy*, XXX. 1.]

But certain of the expressions in this are evidently to be taken figuratively, since Mr. Coffey states, in connection with this and other quotations, that their importance consists in that they establish the existence at a very early date of a tradition associating Brugh na Boinne, the burial-place of the kings of Tara, with the tumuli on the Boyne. The association of particular monuments with the Dagda and other divinities and heroes of Irish mythology implies that the actual persons for whom they were erected had been forgotten, the pagan traditions being probably broken by the introduction of Christianity. The mythological ancestors of the heroes and kings interred at Brugh, who probably were even contemporarily associated with the cemetery, no doubt subsequently overshadowed in tradition the actual persons interred there.

Finally, it seems that the fairy hills may have been actual dwelling-places, fortified or not, of prehistoric peoples. Such were no doubt some of the Picts' houses so fully dealt with by Mr. MacRitchie, though Petrie[A] seems to have considered that many of these were sepulchral in their nature. Such were also the Raths of Ireland and fortified hills, like the White Cater Thun of Forfarshire.

[A: *Anthrop. Mems.*, ii. 216.]

The interior of the mound-dwellings, as described in the stories, is a point to which allusion should be made. Sometimes the mound contains a splendid palace, adorned with gold and silver and precious stones, like the palace of the King of Elf-land in the tale of "Childe Rowland." In the Scandinavian mound-stories we find a curious incident, for they are described as being capable of being raised upon red pillars, and as being so raised when the occupants gave a feast to their neighbours. "There are three hills on the lands of Bubbelgaard in Funen, which are to this day called the Dance-hills, from the following occurrence. A lad named Hans was at service in Bubbelgaard, and as he was coming one evening past the hills, he saw one of them raised on red pillars, and great dancing and much merriment underneath."[A] This feature is met with in several of the stories collected by Keightley, and is made use of in Cruikshank's picture, which forms the frontispiece to that volume. Lastly, in a number of cases there is not merely a habitation, but a vast country underneath the mound. An instance of this occurs in the tale of John Dietrich from the Isle of Ruegen. Under the Nine-hills he found "that there were in that place the most beautiful walks, in which he might ramble along for miles in all directions, without ever finding an end of them, so immensely large was the hill that the little people lived in, and yet outwardly it seemed but a little hill, with a few bushes and trees growing on it."[B]

[A: Quoted by Keightley (p. 9), from Thiele, i. 118.]

[B: Keightley, 178.]

2. The haunts of the fairies may be in caves, and examples of this form of dwelling-place are to be met with in different parts of the world. The Scandinavian hill people live in caves or small hills, and the Elves or dwarfs of La Romagna "dwell in lonely places, far away in the mountains, deep in them, in caves or among old ruins and rocks," as Mr. Leland,[A] who gives a tale respecting these little people, tells us. A Lithuanian tale[B] tells "how the hero, Martin, went into a forest to hunt, accompanied by a smith and a tailor. Finding an empty hut, they took possession of it; the tailor remained in it to cook the dinner, and the others went forth to the chase. When the dinner was almost ready, there came to the hut a very little old man with a very long beard, who piteously begged for food. After receiving it, he sprang on the tailor's neck and beat him almost to death. When the hunters returned, they found their comrade groaning on his couch, complaining of illness, but saying nothing about the bearded dwarf. Next day the smith suffered in a similar way; but

when it came to Martin's turn, he proved too many and too strong for the dwarf, whom he overcame, and whom he fastened by the beard to the stump of a tree. But the dwarf tore himself loose before the hunters came back from the forest and escaped into a cavern. Tracing him by the drops of blood which had fallen from him, the three companions came to the mouth of the cavern, and Martin was lowered into it by the two others. Within it he found three princesses, who had been stolen by three dragons. These dragons he slew, and the princesses and their property he took to the spot above which his comrades kept watch, who hoisted them out of the cavern, but left Martin in it to die. As he wandered about disconsolately, he found the bearded dwarf, whom he slew. And soon afterwards he was conveyed out of the cavern by a flying serpent, and was able to punish his treacherous friends, and to recover the princesses, all three of whom he simultaneously married."

[A: *Etrusco Roman Remains*, p. 222.]

[B: *Folk Lore Record*, i. 85. Mr. Hartland points out to me that this tale, being a Marchen, does not afford quite such good evidence of belief as actually or recently existing as a saga.]

Amongst the Magyars,[A] also, in some localities caves are pointed out as the haunts of fairies, such as the caves in the side of the rock named Budvar, the cave Borza-vara, near the castle of Dame Rapson; another haunt of the fairies is the cave near Almas, and the cold wind known as the "Nemere" is said to blow when the fairy in Almas cave feels cold. On one occasion the plague was raging in this neighbourhood; the people ascribed it to the cold blast emanating from the cave; so they hung shirts before the mouth of the cave and the plague ceased.

[A: Jones and Kropf, *Folk Tales of the Magyars*, pp. xxxvi. *et seq.*]

In a widely distant part of the world, the Battaks-Karo,[A] of the high ground north of Lake Toba in Sumatra, believe in three classes of mysterious beings, one of which closely corresponds with the fairies of Europe. The first group are called Hantous; they are giants and dead Begous (i.e. definitely dead souls), who inhabit Mount Sampouran together with the second group. These are called Omangs; they are dwarfs who marry and reproduce their species, live generally in mountains, and have their feet placed transversely. They must be propitiated, and those making the ascent of Mount Sebayak sacrifice a white hen to them, or otherwise the Omangs would throw stones at them. They carry off men and women, and often keep them for years. They love to dwell amongst stones, and the Roumah Omang, which is one of their favourite habitations, is a cavern. The third group, or Orangs Boumans, resemble ordinary beings, but have the power of making themselves invisible. They come down from the mountains to buy supplies, but have not been seen for some time. Westenberg, from whom this information is quoted, regards the last class as being proscribed Battaks, who have fled for refuge to the mountains. Passing to another continent, the Iroquois[B] have several stories about Pigmies, one of whom, by name Go-ga-ah, lives in a little cave.

[A: *L'Anthropologie*, iv. 83.]

[B: Smith, ***Myths of the Iroquois. American Bureau of Ethnology***, ii. 65.]

3. The little people may occupy a castle or house, or the hill upon which such a building is erected, or a cave under it. Without dwelling upon the Brownies and other similar distinctly household spirits, there are certain classes which must be mentioned in this connection. The Magyar fairies live in castles on lofty mountain peaks. They build them themselves, or inherit them from giants. Kozma enumerates the names of about twenty-three castles which belonged to fairies, and which still exist. Although they have disappeared from earth, they continue to live, even in our days, in caves under their castles, in which caves their treasures lie hidden. The iron gates of Zeta Castle, which have subsided into the ground and disappeared from the surface, open once in every seven years. On one occasion a man went in there, and met two beautiful fairies whom he addressed thus, "How long will you still linger here, my little sisters?" and they replied, "As long as the cows will give warm milk."

Like the interior of some of the mound-dwellings already mentioned, these fairy caves are splendid habitations. "Their subterranean habitations are not less splendid and glittering than were their castles of yore on the mountain peaks. The one at Firtos is a palace resting on solid gold columns. The palace at Tartod and the gorgeous one of Dame Rapson are lighted by three diamond balls, as big as human heads, which hang from golden chains. The treasure which is heaped up in the latter place consists of immense gold bars, golden lions with carbuncle eyes, a golden hen with her brood, and golden casks, filled with gold coin. The treasures of Fairy Helen are kept in a cellar under Kovaszna Castle, the gates of the cellar being guarded by a magic cock. This bird only goes to sleep once in seven years, and anybody who could guess the right moment would be able to scrape no end of diamond crystals from the walls and bring them out with him. The fairies who guard the treasures of the Poganyvar (Pagan Castle) in Marosszek even nowadays come on moonlight nights to bathe in the lake below."[A] In Brittany, "a number of little men, not more than a foot high, dwell under the castle of Morlaix. They live in holes in the ground, whither they may often be seen going, and beating on basins. They possess great treasures, which they sometimes bring out; and if any one pass by at the time, allow him to take one handful, but no more. Should any one attempt to fill his pockets, the money vanishes, and he is instantly assailed by a shower of boxes on the ear from invisible hands."[B] In the Netherlands, the "Gypnissen," "queer little women," lived in a castle which had been reared in a single night.[C] The Ainu have tales of the Poiyaumbe, a name which means literally "little beings residing on the soil" (Mr. Batchelor says that "little" is probably meant to express endearment or admiration, but one may be allowed to doubt this). The Ainu, who is the hero of the story, "comes to a tall mountain with a beautiful house built on its summit. Descending, for his path had always been through the air, by the side of the house, and looking through the chinks of the door, he saw a little man and a little woman sitting beside the fireplace."[D]

[A: ***Folk Tales of the Magyars***, p. xxxviii.]
[B: Grimm, apud Keightley, 441.]
[C: ***Testimony of Tradition***, p. 86.]
[D: ***Folk Lore Journal***, vi. 195.]

4. The little people or fairies occupy rude stone monuments or are connected with their building. In Brittany they are associated with several of the megalithic remains.[A] "At Carnac, near Quiberon," says M. De Cambry, "in the department of Morbihan, on the sea-shore, is the Temple of Carnac, called in Breton 'Ti Goriquet' (House of the Gories), one of the most remarkable Celtic monuments extant. It is composed of more than four thousand large stones, standing erect in an arid plain, where neither tree nor shrub is to be seen, and not even a pebble is to be found in the soil on which they stand. If the inhabitants are asked concerning this wonderful monument, they say it is an old camp of Caesar's, an army turned into stone, or that it is the work of the Crions or Gories. These they describe as little men between two and three feet high, who carried these enormous masses on their hands; for, though

little, they are stronger than giants. Every night they dance around the stones, and woe betide the traveller who approaches within their reach! he is forced to join in the dance, where he is whirled about till, breathless and exhausted, he falls down, amidst the peals of laughter of the Crions. All vanish with the break of day. In the ruins of Tresmalouen dwell the Courils. They are of a malignant disposition, but great lovers of dancing. At night they sport around the Druidical monuments. The unfortunate shepherd that approaches them must dance their rounds with them till cockcrow; and the instances are not few of persons thus ensnared who have been found next morning dead with exhaustion and fatigue. Woe also to the ill-fated maiden who draws near the Couril dance! nine months after, the family counts one member more. Yet so great is the cunning and power of these dwarfs, that the young stranger bears no resemblance to them, but they impart to it the features of some lad of the village."

[A: Keightley, 440.]

In India megalithic remains are also associated with little people. "Dwarfs hold a distinct place in Hindu mythology; they appear sculptured on all temples. Siva is accompanied by a body-guard of dwarfs, one of whom, the three-legged Bhringi, dances nimbly. But coming nearer to Northern legend, the cromlechs and kistvaens which abound over Southern India are believed to have been built by a dwarf race, a cubit high, who could, nevertheless, move and handle the huge stones easily. The villagers call them Pandayar."[A]

[A: *Folk Lore*, iv. 401.]

Mr. Meadows Taylor, speaking of cromlechs in India, says, "Wherever I found them, the same tradition was attached to them, that they were Morie humu, or Mories' houses; these Mories having been dwarfs who inhabited the country before the present race of men." Again, speaking of the cromlechs of Koodilghee, he states, "Tradition says that former Governments caused dwellings of the description alluded to to be erected for a species of human beings called 'Mohories,' whose dwarfish stature is said not to have exceeded a span when standing, and a fist high when in a sitting posture, who were endowed with strength sufficient to roll off large stones with a touch of their thumb." There are, he also tells us, similar traditions attaching to other places, where the dwarfs are sometimes spoken of as Gujaries.[A]

[A: *Jour. Ethnol. Soc.*, 1868-69, p. 157.]

Of stone structures built by fairies or little people for the use of others, may be mentioned the churches built by dwarfs in Scotland and Brittany, and described by Mr. MacRitchie, as also the two following instances, taken from widely distant parts of the globe. In Brittany, the dolmen of Manne-er Hrock (Montaigne de la Fee), at Locmariaquer, is said to have been built by a fairy, in order that a mother might stand upon it and look out for her son's ship.[A] In Fiji the following tale is told about the Nanga or sacred stone enclosure:--"This is the word of our fathers concerning the Nanga. Long ago their fathers were ignorant of it; but one day two strangers were found sitting in the Rara (public square), and they said they had come up from the sea to give them the Nanga. They were little men, and very dark-skinned, and one of them had his face and bust painted red, while the other was painted black. Whether these were gods or men our fathers did not tell us, but it was they who taught our people the Nanga. This was in the old times, when our fathers were living in another land--not in this place, for we are strangers here."[B] It is worthy of note that the term "Nanga" applies not merely to the enclosure, but also to the secret society which held its meetings therein.[C]

[A: *Flint Chips*, p. 104.]

[B: Fison, *Journ. Anthrop. Inst.*, xiv, 14.]

[C: Joske, *Internat. Arch. f. Ethnographie*, viii. 254.]

5. The little people make their dwellings either in the interior of a stone or amongst stones. I am not here alluding to the stones on the sides of mountains which are the doorways to fairy dwellings, but to a closer connection, which will be better understood from some of the following instances than from any lengthy explanation. The Duergas of the Scandinavian Eddas had their dwelling-places in stones, as we are told in the story of Thorston, who "came one day to an open part of the wood, where he saw a great rock, and out a little way from it a dwarf, who was horridly ugly."[A] In Ireland, in Innisbofin, co. Galway, Professor Haddon relates that the men who were quarrying a rock in the neighbourhood of the harbour refused to work at it any longer, as it was so full of "good people" as to be hot.[B] In England the Pixy-house of Devon is in a stone, and a large stone is also connected with the story of the Frensham caldron, though it is not clear that the fairies lived in the rock itself.[C] Oseberrow or Osebury (*vulgo* Rosebury) Rock, in Lulsey, Worcestershire, was, according to tradition, a favourite haunt of the fairies.

[D] In another part of Worcestershire, on the side of the Cotswolds, there is, in a little spinney, a large flat stone, much worn on its under surface, which is called the White Lady's Table. This personage is supposed to take her meals with the fairies at this rock, but what the exact relation of the little people to it as a dwelling-place may be, I have not been able to learn.

[A: Keightley, 70.]

[B: *Folklore*, iv. 49.]

[C: Ritson, 106, quoting Aubrey's *Natural History of Surrey*, iii. 366.]

[D: Allies, *Antiquities and Folk-Lore of Worcestershire*, p.443.]

There is an Iroquois tale of dwarfs, in which the summons to the Pigmies was given by knocking upon a large stone.[A] The little people of Melanesia seem also to be associated in some measure with stones. Speaking of these beings, Mr. Codrington says,[B] "There are certain Vuis having rather the nature of fairies. The accounts of them are vague, but it is argued that they had never left the islands before the introduction of Christianity, and indeed have been seen since. Not long ago there was a woman living at Mota who was the child of one, and a very few years ago a female Vui with a child was seen in Saddle Island. Some of these were called Nopitu, which come invisibly, or possess those with whom they associate themselves. The possessed are called Nopitu. Such persons would lift a cocoa-nut to drink, and native shell money would run out instead of the juice and rattle against their teeth; they would vomit up money, or scratch and shake themselves on a mat, when money would pour from their fingers. This was often seen, and believed to be the doing of a Nopitu. In another manner of manifestation, a Nopitu would make himself known as a party were sitting round an evening fire. A man would hear a voice in his thigh, 'Here am I, give me food.' He would roast a little red yam, and fold it in the corner of his mat. He would soon find it gone, and the Nopitu would begin a song. Its voice was so small and clear and sweet, that once heard it never could be forgotten; but it sang the ordinary Mota songs. Such spirits as these, if seen or found, would disappear beside a stone; they were smaller than the native people, darker, and with long straight hair. But they were mostly unseen, or seen only by those to whom they took a fancy. They were the friendly Trolls or Robin Goodfellows of the islands; a man would find a fine red yam put for him on the seat beside the door, or the money which he paid away returned within his purse. A woman working in her garden heard a voice from the fruit of a gourd asking for some food, and when she pulled up an arum or dug out a yam, another still remained; but when she listened to another spirit's panpipes, the first in his jealousy conveyed away garden and all." Amongst the Australians also supernatural beings dwell amongst the rocks, and the Annamites and Arabians know of fairies living amongst the rocks and hills.[C]

[A: Smith, *Myths of Iroquois, ut supra.*]

[B: *Journ. Anthrop. Inst.*, x. 261.]

[C: Hartland, *Science of Fairy Tales*, p. 351.]

6. The little people may have their habitation in forests or trees. Such were the Skovtrolde, or Wood-Trolls of Thorlacius,[A] who made their home on the earth in great thick woods, and the beings in South Germany who resemble the dwarfs, and are called Wild, Wood, Timber and Moss People.[B] "These generally live together in society, but they sometimes appear singly. They are small in stature, yet somewhat larger than the Elf, being the size of children of three years, grey and old-looking, hairy and clad in moss. Their lives are attached, like those of the Hamadryads, to the trees, and if any one causes by friction the inner bark to loosen, a Wood-woman dies." In Scandinavia there is also a similarity between certain of the Elves and Hamadryads. The Elves "not only frequent trees, but they make an interchange of form with them. In the churchyard of Store Heddinge, in Zeeland, there are the remains of an oak-wood. These, say the common people, are the Elle King's soldiers; by day they are trees, by night valiant soldiers. In the wood of Rugaard, in the same island, is a tree which by night becomes a whole Elle-people, and goes about all alive. It has no leaves upon it, yet it would be very unsafe to go to break or fell it, for the underground people frequently hold their meetings under its branches. There is, in another place, an elder-tree growing in a farmyard, which frequently takes a walk in the twilight about the yard, and peeps in through the window at the children when they are alone. The linden or lime-tree is the favourite haunt of the Elves and cognate beings, and it is not safe to be near it after sunset."[C] In England, the fairies also in some cases frequent the woods, as is their custom in the Isle of Man, and in Wales, where there was formerly, in the park of Sir Robert Vaughan, a celebrated old oak-tree, named Crwben-yr-Ellyl, or the Elf's Hollow Tree. In Formosa[D] there is also a tale of little people inhabiting a wood.

"A young Botan became too ardent in his devotion to a young lady of the tribe, and was slain by her relatives, while, as a warning as to the necessity for love's fervour being kept within bounds, his seven brothers were banished by the chief. The exiles went forth into the depths of the forest, and in their wanderings after a new land they crossed a small clearing, in which a little girl, about a span in height, was seated peeling potatoes. 'Little sister,' they queried, 'how come you here? where is your home?' 'I am not of homes nor parents,' she replied. Leaving her, they went still farther into the forest, and had not gone far when they saw a little man cutting canes, and farther on to the right a curious-looking house, in front of which sat two diminutive women combing their hair. Things looked so queer that the travellers hesitated about approaching nearer, but, eager to find a way out of the forest, they determined in their extremity to question the strange people. The two women, when interrogated, turned sharply round, showing eyes of a flashing red; then looking upward, their eyes became dull and white, and they immediately ran into the house, the doors and windows of which at once vanished, the whole taking the form and appearance of an isolated boulder." Amongst the Maories also we have "te tini ote hakuturi," or "the multitude of the wood-elves," the little people who put the chips all back into the tree Rata had felled and stood it up again, because he had not paid tribute to Tane.[E]

[A: Quoted by Keightley, p. 62.]
[B: Grimm ap. Keightley, p. 230.]
[C: Keightley, p. 92, quoting from Thiele.]
[D: *Folk Lore Journal*, v. 143.]
[E: Tregear, *Journ. Anth. Inst.*, xix. 121.]

7. The association of little people with water as a home is a widespread notion. The Sea-Trows of the Shetlanders inhabit a region of their own at the bottom of the sea. They here respire a peculiar atmosphere, and live in habitations constructed of the choicest submarine productions. They are, however, not always small, but may be of diverse statures, like the Scandinavian Necks. In Germany the Water-Dwarfs are also known. At Seewenheiher, in the Black Forest, a little water-man (*Seemaennlein*) used to come and join the people, work the whole day along with them, and in the evening go back into the lakes.[A] The size of the Breton Korrigs or Korrigan, if we may believe Villemarque in his account of this folk, does not

exceed two feet, but their proportions are most exact, and they have long flowing hair, which they comb out with great care. Their only dress is a long white veil, which they wind round their body. Seen at night or in the dusk of the evening, their beauty is great; but in the daylight their eyes appear red, their hair is white, and their faces wrinkled; hence they rarely let themselves be seen by day. They are fond of music, and have fine voices, but are not much given to dancing. Their favourite haunts are the springs, by which they sit and comb their hair.[B] The Maories also have their Water-Pigmies, the Ponaturi, who are, according to Mr. Tregear, elves, little tiny people, mostly dwellers in water, coming ashore to sleep. [C] "The spirits most commonly met with in African mythology," says Mr. Macdonald, "are water or river spirits, inhabiting deep pools where there are strong eddies and under-currents. Whether they are all even seen now-a-days it is difficult to determine, but they must at one time have either shown themselves willingly, or been dragged from their hiding-places by some powerful magician, for they are one and all described. They are dwarfs, and correspond to the Scottish conception of kelpies or fairies. They are wicked and malevolent beings, and are never credited with a good or generous action. Whatever they possess they keep, and greedily seize upon any one who comes within their reach. 'One of them, the Incanti, corresponds to the Greek Python, and another, called Hiti, appears in the form of a small and very ugly man, and is exceedingly malevolent' (Brownlee). It is certain death to see an Incanti, and no one but the magicians sees them except in dreams, and in that case the magicians are consulted, and advise and direct what is to be done."[D]

[A: Grimm ap. Keightley, p. 261.]

[B: Villemarque, ibid., 431.]

[C: Tregear, *ut supra.*]

[D: *Journ. Anthrop. Inst.*, xx. 124.]

Dr. Nansen, speaking of the Ignerssuit (plural of Ignersuak, which means "great fire"), says that they are for the most part good spirits, inclined to help men. The entrance to their dwellings is on the sea-shore. According to the Eskimo legend, "The first earth which came into existence had neither seas nor mountains, but was quite smooth. When the One above was displeased with the people upon it, He destroyed the world. It burst open, and the people fell down into the rifts and became Ignerssuit and the water poured over everything."[A] The spirits here alluded to appear to be the same as those described by Mr. Boas as Uissuit in his monograph on the Central Eskimo. He describes them as "a strange people that live in the sea. They are dwarfs, and are frequently seen between Iglulik and Netchillik, where the Anganidjen live, an Innuit tribe whose women are in the habit of tracing rings around their eyes. There are men and women among the Uissuit, and they live in deep water, never coming to the surface. When the Innuit wish to see them, they go in their boats to a place where they cannot see the bottom, and try to catch them with hooks which they slowly move up and down. As soon as they get a bite they draw in the line. The Uissuit are thus drawn up; but no sooner do they approach the surface than they dive down headlong again, only their legs having emerged from the water. The Innuit have never succeeded in getting one out of the water."[A]

[A: Nansen, *ut supra*, p. 259.]

[A: *American Bureau of Ethnology*, vi. 612.]

8. Amongst habitations not coming under any of the above categories may be mentioned the moors and open places affected by the Cornish fairies, and lastly the curious residences of the Kirkonwaki or Church-folk of the Finns. "It is an article of faith with the Finns that there dwell under the altar in every church little misshapen beings which they call Kirkonwaki, i.e., Church-folk. When the wives of these little people have a difficult labour, they are relieved if a Christian woman visits them and lays her hand upon them. Such service is always rewarded by a gift of gold and silver."[A] These folk evidently correspond to the Kirkgrims of Scandinavian countries, and the traditions respecting both are probably referable to the practice of foundation sacrifices.

[A: Grimm ap. Keightley, p. 488.]

IV.

The subject of Pigmy races and fairy tales cannot be considered to have been in any sense fully treated without some consideration of a theory which, put forward by various writers and in connection with the legends of diverse countries, has recently been formulated by Mr. MacRitchie in a number of most interesting and suggestive books and papers. An early statement of this theory is to be found in a paper by Mr. J.F. Campbell, in which he stated, "It is somewhat remarkable that traditions still survive in the Highlands of Scotland which seem to be derived from the habits of Scotch tribes like the Lapps in our day. Stories are told in Sutherlandshire about a 'witch' who milked deer; a 'ghost' once became acquainted with a forester, and at his suggestion packed all her plenishing on a herd of deer, when forced to flit by another and a bigger 'ghost;' the green mounds in which 'fairies' are supposed to dwell closely resemble the outside of Lapp huts. The fairies themselves are not represented as airy creatures in gauze wings and spangles, but they appear in tradition as small cunning people, eating and drinking, living close at hand in their green mound, stealing children and cattle, milk and food, from their bigger neighbours. They are uncanny, but so are the Lapps. My own opinion is that these Scotch traditions relate to the tribes who made kitchen-middens and lake-dwellings in Scotland, and that they were allied to Lapps."[A] Such in essence is Mr. MacRitchie's theory, which has been so admirably summarised by Mr. Jacobs in the first of that series of fairy-tale books which has added a new joy to life, that I shall do myself the pleasure of quoting his statement in this place. He says: "Briefly put, Mr. MacRitchie's view is that the elves, trolls, and fairies represented in popular tradition are really the mound-dwellers, whose remains have been discovered in some abundance in the form of green hillocks, which have been artificially raised over a long and low passage leading to a central chamber open to the sky. Mr. MacRitchie shows that in several instances traditions about trolls or 'good people' have attached themselves to mounds which long afterwards, on investigation, turned out to be evidently the former residence of men of smaller build than the mortals of to-day. He goes on further to identify these with the Picts-- fairies are called 'Pechs' in Scotland--and other early races, but with these ethnological equations we need not much concern ourselves. It is otherwise with the mound traditions and their relation, if not to fairy tales in general, to tales about fairies, trolls, elves, &c. These are very few in number, and generally bear the character of anecdotes. The fairies, &c., steal a child; they help a wanderer to a drink and then disappear into a green hill; they help cottagers with their work at night, but disappear if their presence is noticed; human midwives are asked to help fairy mothers; fairy maidens marry ordinary men, or girls marry and live with fairy husbands. All such things may have happened and bear no such *a priori* marks of impossibility as speaking animals, flying through the air, and similar incidents of the folk-tale pure and simple. If, as archaeologists tell us, there was once a race of men in Northern Europe very short and hairy, that dwelt in underground chambers artificially concealed by green hillocks, it does not seem unlikely that odd survivors of the race should have lived on after they had been conquered and nearly exterminated by Aryan invaders, and should occasionally have performed something like the pranks told of fairies and trolls."[B] In the same place, and also in another article,[C] the writer just quoted has applied this theory to the explanation of the story of "Childe Rowland."

[A: *Journ. Ethnol. Soc.*, 1869-70, p. 325.]

[B: *English Fairy Tales*, p. 241.]

[C: *Folk Lore*, ii. 126.]

Mr. MacRitchie has, in another paper,[A] collected a number of instances of the use of the word **Sith** in connection with hillocks and tumuli, which are the resort of the fairies. Here also he discusses the possible connection of that word with that of **Tshud**, the title of the vanished supernatural inhabitants of the land amongst the Finns and other "Altaic" Turanian tribes of Russia, as in other places he has endeavoured to trace a connection between the Finns and the Feinne. Into these etymological questions I have no intention to enter, since I am not qualified to do so, nor is it necessary, as they have been fully dealt with by Mr. Nutt, whose opinion on this point is worthy of all attention.[B] But it may be permitted to me to inquire how far Mr. MacRitchie's views tally with the facts mentioned in the foregoing section. I shall therefore allude to a few points which appear to me to show that the origin of the belief in fairies cannot be settled in so simple a manner as has been suggested, but is a question of much greater complexity--one in which, as Mr. Tylor says, more than one mythic element combines to make up the whole.

[A: *Journ. Roy. Soc. Antiq. Ireland*, iii. 367.]

[A: *Folk and Hero Tales from Argyleshire*, p. 420.]

(1.) In the first place, then, it seems clear, so far as our present knowledge teaches us, that there never was a really Pigmy race inhabiting the northern parts of Scotland.

The scanty evidence which we have on this point, so far as it goes, proves the truth of this assertion. Mr. Carter Blake found in the Muckle Heog of the Island of Unst, one of the Shetlands, together with stone vessels, human interments of persons of considerable stature and of great muscular strength. Speaking of the Keiss skeletons, Professor Huxley says that the males are, the one somewhat above, and the other probably about the average stature; while the females are short, none exceeding five feet two inches or three inches in height.[A] And Dr. Garson, treating of the osteology of the ancient inhabitants of the Orkneys, says that the female skeleton which he examined was about five feet two inches in height, i.e., about the mean height of the existing races of England.[B] There is no evidence that Lapps and Eskimo ever visited these parts of the world; and if they did, as we have seen, their stature, though stunted, cannot fairly be described as pigmy. Even if we grant that the stature of the early races did not average more than five feet two inches, which, by the way, was the height of the great Napoleon, it is more than doubtful whether it fell so far short of that of succeeding races as to cause us to imagine that it gave rise to tales about a race of dwarfs.

[A: Laing, *Prehistoric Remains of Caithness*, p. 101.]

[B: *Journ. Anthrop. Inst.*, xiii. 60.]

(2.) The mounds with which the tales of little people are associated have not, in many cases, been habitations, but were natural or sepulchral in their nature. It may, of course, be argued that the story having once arisen in connection with one kind of mound, may, by a process easy to understand, have been transferred to other hillocks similar in appearance, though diverse in nature. It is difficult to see, however, how this could have occurred in Yorkshire and other parts of England, where it is not argued that the stunted inhabitants of the North ever penetrated. It is still more difficult to explain how similar legends can have originated in America in connection with mounds, since there never were Pigmy races in that continent.

(3.) The rude and simple arrangements of the interior of these mound dwellings might have, in the process of time, become altered into the gorgeous halls, decked with gold and silver and precious stones, as we find them in the stories; they might even, though this is much more difficult to understand, have become possessed of the capacity for being raised upon red pillars. But there is one pitch to which, I think, they could never have attained, and that is the importance which they assume when they become the external covering of a large and extensive tract of underground country. Here we are brought face to face with a totally different explanation, to which I shall recur in due course.

(4.) The little people are not by any means associated entirely with mounds, as the foregoing section is largely intended to show. Their habitations may be in or amongst stones, in caves, under the water, in trees, or amongst the glades of a forest; they may dwell on mountains, on moors, or even under the altars of churches. We may freely grant that some of these habitations fall into line with Mr. MacRitchie's theory, but they are not all susceptible of such an explanation.

(5.) The association of giants and dwarfs in certain places, even the confusion of the two races, seems somewhat difficult of explanation by this theory. In Ireland the distinction between the two classes is sharper than in other places, since, as Sir William Wilde pointed out, whilst every green rath in that island is consecrated to the fairies or "good people," the remains attributed to the giants are of a different character and probably of a later date. In some places, however, a mound similar to those often connected with fairies is associated with a giant, as is the case at Sessay parish, near Thirsk,[A] and at Fyfield in Wiltshire. The chambered tumulus at Luckington is spoken of as the Giant's Caves, and that at Nempnet in Somersetshire as the Fairy's Toot. In Denmark, tumuli seem to be described indifferently as Zettestuer (Giants' Chambers) or Troldestuer (Fairies' Chambers).[B] In "Beowulf" a chambered tumulus is described, in the recesses of which were treasures watched over for three hundred years by a dragon. This barrow was of stone, and the work of giants.

Seah on enta geweorc,   Looked on the giant's work, hu etha stan-bogan, how the stone arches, stapulinn-faeste,   on pillars fast, ece eoreth-reced   the eternal earth-house innan healde.   held within.

[A: *Folk Lore*, i. 130.]

[B: *Flint Chips*, p. 412.]

The mounds have sometimes been made by giants and afterwards inhabited by dwarfs, as in the case of the Nine-hills, already alluded to. In others, they are at the same time inhabited by giants, dwarfs, and others, as in the story of the Dwarf's Banquet,[A] and still more markedly in the Wunderberg. "The celebrated Wunderberg, or Underberg, on the great moor near Salzburg, is the chief haunt of the Wild-women. The Wunderberg is said to be quite hollow, and supplied with stately palaces, churches, monasteries, gardens, and springs of gold and silver. Its inhabitants, beside the Wild-women, are little men, who have charge of the treasures it contains, and who at midnight repair to Salzburg to perform their devotions in the cathedral; giants, who used to come to the church of Groedich and exhort the people to lead a godly and pious life; and the great Emperor Charles V., with golden crown and sceptre, attended by knights and lords. His grey beard has twice encompassed the table at which he sits, and when it has the third time grown round it, the end of the world and the appearance of the Antichrist will take place."[B]

[A: Grimm ap. Keightley, 130.]

[B: Grimm ap. Keightley, 234.]

In the folk-tales of the Magyars we meet with a still more remarkable confusion between these two classes of beings. Some of the castles described in these stories are inhabited by giants, others by fairies. Again, the giants marry; their wives are fairies, so are their daughters. They had no male issue, as their race was doomed to extermination. They fall in love, and are fond of courting. Near Bikkfalva, in Haromszek, the people still point out the "Lover's Bench" on a rock where the amorous giant of Csigavar used to meet his sweetheart, the "fairy of Veczeltetoe."[A]

[A: *Folk Tales of the Magyars*, p. xxix.]

(6.) Tales of little people are to be found in countries where there never were any Pigmy races. Not to deal with other, and perhaps more debatable districts, we find an excellent example of this in North America. Besides the instances mentioned in the foregoing section, the following may be mentioned. Mr. Leland, speaking of the Un-a-games-suk, or Indian spirits of the rocks and streams, says that these beings enter far more largely, deeply, and socially into the life and faith of the Indians than elves or fairies ever did into those of the Aryan race.[A] In his Algonquin Legends the same author also alludes to small people.

[A: *Memoirs*, i. 34.]

Dr. Brinton tells me that the Micmacs have tales of similar Pigmies, whom they call Wig[)u]l[)a]d[)u]mooch, who tie people with cords during their sleep, &c. Mr. L.L. Frost, of Susanville, Lassen County, California, tells us how, when he requested an Indian to gather and bring in all the arrow-points he could find, the Indian declared them to be "no good," that they had been made by the lizards. Whereupon Mr. Frost drew from him the following lizard-story. "There was a time when the lizards were little men, and the arrow-points which are now found were shot by them at the grizzly bear. The bears could talk then, and would eat the little men whenever they could catch them. The arrows of the little men were so small that they would not kill the bears when shot into them, and only served to enrage them." The Indian could not tell how the little men became transformed into lizards.[A] Again, the Shoshones of California dread their infants being changed by Ninumbees or dwarfs.[B]

[A: *Folk Lore Journal*, vii. 24.]

[B: Hartland, *ut supra*, p. 351.]

Finally, every one has read about the Pukwudjies, "the envious little people, the fairies, the pigmies," in the pages of Longfellow's "Hiawatha."[A] It ought to be mentioned that Mr. Leland states that the red-capped, scanty-shirted elf of the Algonquins was obtained from the Norsemen; but if, as he says, the idea of little people has sunk so deeply into the Indian mind, it cannot in any large measure have been derived from this source.[B]

[A: xviii.]

[B: *Etrusco Roman Remains*, p. 162.]

(7.) The stunted races whom Mr. MacRitchie considers to have formed the subjects of the fairy legend have themselves tales of little people. This is true especially of the Eskimo, as will have been already noticed, a fact to which my attention was called by Mr. Hartland.

For the reasons just enumerated, I am unable to accept Mr. MacRitchie's theory as a complete explanation of the fairy question, but I am far from desirous of under-estimating the value and significance of his work. Mr. Tylor, as I have already mentioned, states, in a sentence which may yet serve as a motto for a work on the whole question of the origin of the fairy myth, that "various different facts have given rise to stories of giants and dwarfs, more than one mythic element perhaps combining to form a single legend--a result perplexing in the extreme to the mythological interpreter."[A] And I think it may be granted that Mr. MacRitchie has gone far to show that one of these mythic elements, one strand in the twisted cord of fairy my-thology, is the half-forgotten memory of skulking aborigines, or, as Mr. Nutt well puts it, the "distorted recollections of alien and inimical races." But it is not the only one. It is far from being my intention to endeavour to deal exhaustively with the difficult question of the origin of fairy tales. Knowledge and the space permissible in an introduction such as this would alike fail me in such a task. It may, however, be permissible to mention a few points which seem to impress themselves upon one in making a study of the stories with which I have been dealing. In the first place, one can scarcely fail to notice how much in common there is between the tales of the little people and the accounts of that underground world, which, with so many races, is the habitation of the souls of the departed. Dr. Callaway has already drawn attention to this point in connection with the ancestor-worship of the Amazulu. [B] He says, "It may be worth while to note the curious coincidence of thought among the Amazulu regarding the Amatongo or Abapansi, and that of the Scotch and Irish regarding the fairies or 'good people.' For instance, the 'good people' of the Irish have assigned to them, in many respects the same motives and actions as the Amatongo. They call the living to join them, that is, by death; they cause dis-ease which common doctors cannot understand nor cure; they have their feelings, interests, partialities, and antipathies, and contend with each other about the living. The common people call them their friends or people, which is equivalent to the term **abakubo** given to the Amatongo. They reveal themselves in the form of the dead, and it appears to be supposed that the dead become 'good people,' as the dead among the Amazulu become Amatongo; and in funeral processions of the 'good people' which some have professed to see, are recognised the forms of those who have just died, as Umkatshana saw his relatives amongst the Abapansi. The power of holding communion with the 'good people' is consequent on an illness, just as the power to divine amongst the natives of this country. So also in the Highland tales, a boy who had been carried away by the fairies, on his return to his own home speaks of them as 'our folks,' which is equivalent to **abakwetu**, applied to the Amatongo, and among the Highlands they are called the 'good people' and 'the folk.' They are also said to 'live underground,' and are therefore Abapansi or subterranean. They are also, like the Abapansi, called ancestors. Thus the Red Book of Clanranald is said not to have been dug up, but to have been found on the moss; it seemed as if the ancestors sent it." There are other points which make in the same direction. The soul is supposed by various races to be a little man, an idea which at once links the manes of the departed with Pigmy people. Thus Dr. Nansen tells us that amongst the Eskimo a man has many souls. The largest dwell in the larynx and in the left side, and are tiny men about the size of a sparrow. The other souls dwell in other parts of the body, and are the size of a finger-joint.[C] And the Macusi Indians[D] believe that although the body will decay, "the man in our eyes" will not die, but wander about; an idea which is met with even in Europe, and which perhaps gives us a clue to the conception of smallness in size of the shades of the dead. Again, the belief that the soul lives near the resting-place of its body is widespread, and at least comparable with, if not equivalent to, the idea that the little people of Scotland, Ireland, Brittany, and India live in the sepulchral mounds or cromlechs of those countries. Closely connected with this is the idea of the underground world, peopled by the souls of the departed like the Abapansi, the widespread nature of which idea is shown by Dr. Tylor. "To take one example, in which the more limited idea seems to have preceded the more extensive, the Finns,[E] who feared the ghost of the departed as unkind, harmful beings, fancied them dwelling with their bodies in the grave, or else, with what Castren thinks a later philosophy, assigned them their dwelling in the subterranean Tuonela. Tuonela was like this upper earth; the sun shone there, there was no lack of land and water, wood and field, tilth and meadow; there were bears and wolves, snakes and pike, but all things were of a hurtful, dismal kind; the woods dark and swarming with wild beasts, the water black, the cornfields bearing seed of snake's teeth; and there stern, pitiless old Tuoni, and his grim wife and son, with the hooked fingers with iron points, kept watch and ward over the dead lest they should escape."

[A: *Primitive Culture*, i. 388.]

[B: *Religious System of the Amazulu*, p. 226.]

[C: Nansen, *ut supra*, p. 227.]

[D: Tylor, *ut supra*, i. 431.]

[E: Tylor, *ut supra*, ii. 80.]

It is impossible not to see a connection between such conceptions as these and the underground habitations of the little people entered by the green mound which covered the bones of the dead. But the underground world was not only associated with the shades of the departed; it was in many parts of the world the place whence races had their origin, and here also we meet in at least one instance known to me with the conception of a little folk. A very widespread legend in Europe, and especially in Scandinavia, according to Dr. Nansen, tells how the underground or invisible people came into existence. "The Lord one day paid a visit to Eve as she was busy washing her children. All those who were not yet washed she hurriedly hid in cellars and corners and under big vessels, and presented the others to the Visitor. The Lord asked if these were all, and she answered 'Yes;' whereupon He replied, 'Then those which are *dulde* (hidden) shall remain *hulde* (concealed, invisible). And from them the huldre-folk are sprung."[A] There is also the widespread story of an origin underground, as amongst the Wasabe, a sub-gens of the Omahas, who believe that their ancestors were made under the earth and subsequently came to the surface.[B] There is a similar story amongst the Z[=u]nis of Western New Mexico. In journeying to their present place of habitation, they passed through four worlds, all in the interior of this, the passage way from darkness to light being through a large reed. From the inner world they were led by the two little war-gods, Ah-ai-[=u]-ta and M[=a]-[=a]-s[=e]-we, twin brothers, sons of the Sun, who were sent by the Sun to bring this people to his presence.[C] From these stories it would appear that the underground world, whether looked upon as the habitation of the dead or the place of origination of nations, is connected with the conception of little races and people. That it is thus responsible for some portion of the conception of fairies seems to me to be more than probable.

[A: Nansen, *ut supra*, p. 262.]

[B: Dorset, *Omaha Sociology. American Bureau of Ethnology*, iii. 211.]

[C: Stevenson, *Religious Life of Zuni Child. American Bureau of Ethnology*,

v. 539.]

It is hardly necessary to allude to those spirits which animistic ideas have attached amongst other objects and places, to trees and wells. They are fully dealt with in Dr. Tylor's pages, and must not be forgotten in connection with the present question.

To sum up, then, it appears as if the idea, so widely diffused, of little, invisible, or only sometimes visible, people, is of the most complex nature. From the darkness which shrouds it, however, it is possible to discern some rays of light. That the souls of the departed, and the underground world which they inhabit, are largely responsible for it, is, I hope, rendered probable by the facts which I have brought forward. That animistic ideas have played an important part in the evolution of the idea of fairy peoples, is not open to doubt. That to these conceptions were superadded many features really derived from the actions of aboriginal races hiding before the destroying might of their invaders, and this not merely in these islands, but in many parts of the world, has been, I think, demonstrated by the labours of the gentleman whose theory I have so often alluded to. But the point upon which it is desired to lay stress is that the features derived from aboriginal races are only one amongst many sources. Possibly they play an important part, but scarcely, I think, one so important as Mr. MacRitchie would have us believe.

A PHILOLOGICAL ESSAY

Concerning the PYGMIES, THE CYNOCEPHALI, THE SATYRS and SPHIN-GES OF THE ANCIENTS,

Wherein it will appear that they were all either APES or MONKEYS; and not MEN, as formerly pretended.

By Edward Tyson M.D.

A Philological Essay Concerning the PYGMIES OF THE ANCIENTS.

Having had the Opportunity of Dissecting this remarkable Creature, which not only in the *outward shape* of the Body, but likewise in the structure of many of the Inward Parts, so nearly resembles a Man, as plainly appears by the *Anatomy* I have here given of it, it suggested the Thought to me, whether this sort of *Animal*, might not give the Foundation to the Stories of the *Pygmies* and afford an occasion not only to the *Poets*, but *Historians* too, of inventing the many Fables and wonderful and merry Relations, that are transmitted down to us concerning them? I must confess, I could never before entertain any other Opinion about them, but that the whole was a *Fiction*: and as the first Account we have of them, was from a *Poet*, so that they were only a Creature of the Brain, produced by a warm and wanton Imagination, and that they never had any Existence or Habitation elsewhere.

In this Opinion I was the more confirmed, because the most diligent Enquiries of late into all the Parts of the inhabited World, could never discover any such *Puny* diminutive *Race* of *Mankind*. That they should be totally destroyed by the *Cranes*, their Enemies, and not a Straggler here and there left remaining, was a Fate, that even those *Animals* that are constantly preyed upon by others, never undergo. Nothing therefore appeared to me more Fabulous and Romantick, than their *History*, and the Relations about them, that *Antiquity* has delivered to us. And not only *Strabo* of old, but our greatest Men of Learning of late, have wholly exploded them, as a mere *figment*; invented only to amuse, and divert the Reader with the Comical Narration of their Atchievements, believing that there were never any such Creatures in Nature.

This opinion had so fully obtained with me, that I never thought it worth the Enquiry, how they came to invent such Extravagant Stories: Nor should I now, but upon the Occasion of Dissecting this *Animal*: For observing that 'tis call'd even to this day in the *Indian* or *Malabar* Language, *Orang-Outang*, i.e. a *Man* of the *Woods*, or *Wild-men*; and being brought from *Africa*, that part of the World, where the *Pygmies* are said to inhabit; and it's present *Stature* likewise tallying so well with that of the *Pygmies* of the Ancients; these Considerations put me upon the search, to inform my self farther about them, and to examine, whether I could meet with any thing that might illustrate their *History*. For I thought it strange, that if the whole was but a meer Fiction, that so many succeeding Generations should be so fond of preserving a *Story*, that had no Foundation at all in Nature; and that the *Ancients* should trouble themselves so much about them. If therefore I can make out in this *Essay*, that there were such *Animals* as *Pygmies*; and that they were not a *Race* of *Men*, but *Apes*; and can discover the *Authors*, who have forged all, or most of the idle Stories concerning them; and shew how the Cheat in after Ages has been carried on, by embalming the Bodies of *Apes*, then exposing them for the *Men* of the Country, from whence they brought them: If I can do this, I shall think my time not wholly lost, nor the trouble altogether useless, that I have had in this Enquiry.

My Design is not to justifie all the Relations that have been given of this *Animal*, even by Authors of reputed Credit; but, as far as I can, to distinguish Truth from Fable; and herein, if what I assert amounts to a Probability, 'tis all I pretend to. I shall accordingly endeavour to make it appear, that not only the *Pygmies* of the Ancients, but also the *Cynocephali*, and *Satyrs* and *Sphinges* were only *Apes* or *Monkeys*, not *Men*, as they have been represented. But the Story of the *Pygmies* being the greatest Imposture, I shall chiefly concern my self about them, and shall be more concise on the others, since they will not need so strict an Examination.

We will begin with the Poet **Homer**, who is generally owned as the first Inventor of the Fable of the **Pygmies**, if it be a Fable, and not a true Story, as I believe will appear in the Account I shall give of them. Now **Homer** only mentions them in a **Simile**, wherein he compares the Shouts that the **Trojans** made, when they were going to joyn Battle with the **Graecians**, to the great Noise of the **Cranes**, going to fight the **Pygmies**: he saith,[A]

[Greek: Ai t' epei oun cheimona phygon, kai athesphaton ombron Klangae tai ge petontai ep' okeanoio rhoaon 'Andrasi pygmaioisi phonon kai kaera pherousai.] i.e.

Quae simul ac fugere Imbres, Hyememque Nivalem Cum magno Oceani clangore ferantur ad undas Pygmaeis pugnamque Viris, caedesque ferentes.

[A: *Homer. Iliad*. lib. 3. ver. 4.]

Or as **Helius Eobanus Hessus** paraphrases the whole.[A]

Postquam sub Ducibus digesta per agmina stabant Quaeque fuis, Equitum turmae, Peditumque Cohortes, Obvia torquentes Danais vestigia Troes Ibant, sublato Campum clamore replentes: Non secus ac cuneata Gruum sublime volantum Agmina, dum fugiunt Imbres, ac frigora Brumae, Per Coelum matutino clangore feruntur, Oceanumque petunt, mortem exitiumque cruentum Irrita Pigmaeis moturis arma ferentes.

[A: *Homeri Ilias Latino Carmine reddita ab Helio Eobano Hesso*.]

By [Greek: andrasi pygmaioisi] therefore, which is the Passage upon which they have grounded all their fabulous Relations of the **Pygmies**, why may not **Homer** mean only **Pygmies** or **Apes** like **Men**. Such an Expression is very allowable in a **Poet**, and is elegant and significant, especially since there is so good a Foundation in Nature for him to use it, as we have already seen, in the ***Anatomy of the Orang-Outang***. Nor is a **Poet** tied to that strictness of Expression, as an **Historian** or **Philosopher**; he has the liberty of pleasing the Reader's Phancy, by Pictures and Representations of his own. If there be a becoming likeness, 'tis all that he is accountable for. I might therefore here make the same **Apology** for him, as **Strabo**[A] do's on another account for his **Geography**, [Greek: ou gar kat' agnoian ton topikon legetai, all' haedonaes kai terpseos charin]. That he said it, not thro' Ignorance, but to please and delight: Or, as in another place he expresses himself,[B] [Greek: ou gar kat' agnoian taes istorias hypolaepteon genesthai touto, alla tragodias charin]. *Homer* did not make this slip thro' Ignorance of the true *History*, but for the Beauty of his *Poem*. So that tho' he calls them *Men Pygmies*, yet he may mean no more by it, than that they were like *Men*. As to his Purpose, 'twill serve altogether as well, whether this bloody Battle be fought between the *Cranes* and *Pygmaean Men*, or the *Cranes* and *Apes*, which from their Stature he calls *Pygmies*, and from their shape *Men*; provided that when the *Cranes* go to engage, they make a mighty terrible noise, and clang enough to fright these little *Wights* their mortal Enemies. To have called them only *Apes*, had been flat and low, and lessened the grandieur of the Battle. But this *Periphrasis* of them, [Greek: andres pygmaioi], raises the Reader's Phancy, and surprises him, and is more becoming the Language of an Heroic Poem.

[A: *Strabo Geograph*. lib. 1. p.m. 25.]

[B: *Strabo* ibid. p.m. 30.]

But how came the *Cranes* and *Pygmies* to fall out? What may be the Cause of this Mortal Feud, and constant War between them? For *Brutes*, like *Men*, don't war upon one another, to raise and encrease their Glory, or to enlarge their Empire. Unless I can acquit my self herein, and assign some probable Cause hereof, I may incur the same Censure as *Strabo*[A] passed on several of the *Indian Historians*, [Greek: enekainisan de kai taen 'Omaerikaen ton Pygmaion geranomachin trispithameis eipontes], for reviewing the *Homerical* Fight of the *Cranes* and *Pygmies*, which he looks upon only as a fiction of the Poet. But this had been very unbecoming *Homer* to take a *Simile* (which is designed for illustration) from what had no Foundation in Nature. His *Betrachomyomachia*, 'tis true, was a meer Invention, and never otherwise esteemed: But his *Geranomachia* hath all the likelyhood of a true Story. And therefore I shall enquire now what may be the just Occasion of this Quarrel.

[A: *Strabo Geograph*. lib. 2. p.m. 48.]

Athenaeus[A] out of *Philochorus*, and so likewise *AElian*[B], tell us a Story, That in the Nation of the *Pygmies* the Male-line failing, one *Gerana* was the Queen; a Woman of an admired Beauty, and whom the Citizens worshipped as a

Goddess; but she became so vain and proud, as to prefer her own, before the Beauty of all the other Goddesses, at which they grew enraged; and to punish her for her Insolence, Athenaeus tells us that it was *Diana*, but *AElian* saith 'twas *Juno* that transformed her into a *Crane*, and made her an Enemy to the *Pygmies* that worshipped her before. But since they are not agreed which Goddess 'twas, I shall let this pass.

[A: *Athenaei Deipnosoph*. lib. 9 p.m. 393.]

[B: *AElian. Hist. Animal*. lib. 15. cap. 29.]

Pomponius Mela will have it, and I think some others, that these cruel Engagements use to happen, upon the *Cranes* coming to devour the *Corn* the *Pygmies* had sowed; and that at last they became so victorious, as not only to destroy their Corn, but them also: For he tells us,[A] *Fuere interius Pygmaei, minutum genus, & quod pro satis frugibus contra Grues dimicando, defecit*. This may seem a reasonable Cause of a Quarrel; but it not being certain that the *Pygmies* used to sow *Corn*, I will not insist on this neither.

[A: *Pomp. Mela de situ Orbis*, lib. 3. cap. 8.]

Now what seems most likely to me, is the account that *Pliny* out of *Megasthenes*, and *Strabo* from *Onesicritus* give us; and, provided I be not obliged to believe or justifie *all* that they say, I could rest satisfied in great part of their Relation: For *Pliny*[B] tells us, *Veris tempore universo agmine ad mare descendere, & Ova, Pullosque earum Alitum consumere*: That in the Spring-time the whole drove of the *Pygmies* go down to the Sea side, to devour the *Cranes* Eggs and their young Ones. So likewise *Onesicritus*,[B] [Greek: Pros de tous trispithamous polemon einai tais Geranois (hon kai Homaeron daeloun) kai tois Perdixin, ous chaenomegetheis einai; toutous d' eklegein auton ta oa, kai phtheirein; ekei gar ootokein tas Geranous; dioper maedamou maed' oa euriskesthai Geranon, maet' oun neottia;] i.e. *That there is a fight between the* Pygmies *and the* Cranes (*as* Homer *relates*) *and the* Partridges *which are as big as* Geese; *for these* Pygmies *gather up their Eggs, and destroy them; the* Cranes *laying their Eggs there; and neither their Eggs, nor their Nests, being to be found any where else*. 'Tis plain therefore from them, that the Quarrel is not out of any *Antipathy* the *Pygmies* have to the *Cranes*, but out of love to their own Bellies. But the *Cranes* finding their Nests to be robb'd, and their young Ones prey'd on by these Invaders, no wonder that they should so sharply engage them; and the least they could do, was to fight to the utmost so mortal an Enemy. Hence, no doubt, many a bloody Battle happens, with various success to the Combatants; sometimes with great slaughter of the *long-necked Squadron*; sometimes with great effusion of *Pygmaean* blood. And this may well enough, in a *Poet's* phancy, be magnified, and represented as a dreadful War; and no doubt of it, were one a *Spectator* of it, 'twould be diverting enough.

    [A: *Plinij. Hist. Nat.* lib. 7. cap. 2. p.m. 13.]

    [B: *Strab. Geograph*. lib. 15. pag. 489.]

    -----Si videas hoc

Gentibus in nostris, risu quatiere: sed illic,

Quanquam eadem assidue spectantur Praelia, ridet

Nemo, ubi tota cohors pede non est altior uno.[A]

    [A: *Juvenal. Satyr*. 13 vers. 170.]

This Account therefore of these Campaigns renewed every year on this Provocation between the *Cranes* and the *Pygmies*, contains nothing but what a cautious Man may believe; and *Homer's Simile* in likening the great shouts of the *Trojans* to the Noise of the *Cranes*, and the Silence of the *Greeks* to that of the *Pygmies*, is very admirable and delightful. For *Aristotle*[B] tells us, That the *Cranes*, to avoid the hardships of the Winter, take a Flight out of *Scythia* to the *Lakes* about the *Nile*, where the *Pygmies* live, and where 'tis very likely the *Cranes* may lay their Eggs and breed, before they return. But these rude *Pygmies* making too bold with them, what could the *Cranes* do less for preserving their Off-spring than fight them; or at least by their mighty Noise, make a shew as if they would. This is but what we may observe in all other Birds. And thus far I think our *Geranomachia* or *Pygmaeomachia* looks like a true Story; and there is nothing in *Homer* about it, but what is credible. He only expresses himself, as a *Poet* should do; and if Readers will mistake his meaning, 'tis not his fault.

    [B: *Aristotle. Hist. Animal*. lib. 8. cap. 15. Edit. Scalig.]

'Tis not therefore the *Poet* that is to be blamed, tho' they would father it all on him; but the fabulous *Historians* in after Ages, who have so odly drest up this Story by their fantastical Inventions, that there is no knowing the truth, till one hath pull'd off those Masks and Visages, wherewith they have disguised it. For tho' I can believe *Homer*, that there is a fight between the *Cranes* and *Pygmies*, yet I think I am no ways obliged to imagine, that when the *Pygmies* go to these Campaigns to fight the *Cranes*, that they ride upon *Partridges*, as *Athenaeas* from *Basilis* an *Indian Historian* tells us; for, saith he,[A] [Greek: Basilis de en toi deuteroi ton Indikon, oi mikroi, phaesin, andres oi tais Geranois diapolemountes Perdixin och-aemati chrontai;]. For presently afterwards he tells us from *Menecles*, that the *Pyg-mies* not only fight the *Cranes*, but the *Partridges* too, [Greek: Meneklaes de en protae taes synagogaes oi pygmaioi, phaesi, tois perdixi, kai tais Geranois polemou-si]. This I could more readily agree to, because *Onesicritus*, as I have quoted him already confirms it; and gives us the same reason for this as for fighting the *Cranes*, because they rob their Nests. But whether these *Partridges* are as big as *Geese*, I leave as a *Quaere*.

[A: *Athenaei Deipnesoph*. lib. p. 9. m. 390.]

Megasthenes methinks in *Pliny* mounts the *Pygmies* for this expedition much better, for he sets them not on a *Pegasus* or *Partridges*, but on *Rams* and *Goats*: *Fama est* (saith Pliny[A]) insedentes Arietum Caprarumque dorsis, ar-matis sagittis, veris tempore universo agmine ad mare descendere. *And* Onesicritus *in Strabo tells us, That a* Crane has been often observed to fly from those parts with a brass Sword fixt in him, [Greek: pleistakis d' ekpiptein geranon chalkaen echousan akida apo ton ekeithen plaegmaton.][B] But whether the *Pygmies* do wear Swords, may be doubted. 'Tis true, *Ctesias* tells us,[C] That the *King* of *India* every fifth year sends fifty Thousand Swords, besides abundance of other Weapons, to the Nation of the *Cynocephali*, (a fort of *Monkeys*, as I shall shew) that live in those Countreys, but higher up in the Mountains: But he makes no mention of any such Presents to the poor *Pygmies*; tho' he assures us, that no less than three Thousand of these *Pygmies* are the *Kings* constant Guards: But withal tells us, that they are excellent *Archers*, and so perhaps by dispatching their Enemies at a distance, they may have no need of such Weapons to lye dangling by their sides. I may therefore be mistaken in rendering [Greek: akida] a Sword; it may be any other sharp pointed Instrument or Weapon, and upon second Thoughts, shall suppose it a sort of Arrow these cunning *Archers* use in these Engagements.

[A: ***Plinij. Nat. Hist.*** lib. 7. cap. 2. p. 13.]

[B: ***Strabo Geograph.*** lib. 15. p. 489.]

[C: ***Vide Photij. Biblioth.***]

These, and a hundred such ridiculous *Fables*, have the *Historians* invented of the *Pygmies*, that I can't but be of *Strabo*'s mind,[A] [Greek: Rhadion d' an tis Haesiodio, kai Homaeroi pisteuseien haeroologousi, kai tois tragikois poiaetais, hae Ktaesiai te kai Haerodotoi, kai Hellanikoi, kai allois toioutois;] i.e. *That one may sooner believe* Hesiod, *and* Homer, *and the* Tragick Poets *speaking of their* Hero's, *than* Ctesias *and* Herodotus *and* Hellanicus *and such like*. So ill an Opinion had *Strabo* of the *Indian Historians* in general, that he censures them *all* as fabulous;[B] [Greek: Hapantes men toinun hoi peri taes Indikaes grapsantes hos epi to poly pseudologoi gegonasi kath' hyperbolaen de Daeimachos; ta de deutera legei Megasthenaes, Onaesikritos te kai Nearchos, kai alloi toioutoi;] i.e. *All who have wrote of* India *for the most part, are fabulous, but in the highest degree* Daimachus; *then* Megasthenes, Onesicritus, *and* Nearchus, *and such like*. And as if it had been their greatest Ambition to excel herein, *Strabo*[C] brings in *Theopompus*, as bragging, [Greek: Hoti kai mythous en tais Historiais erei kreitton, ae hos Haerodotos, kai Ktaesias, kai Hellanikos, kai hoi ta Hindika syngrapsantes;] *That he could foist in Fables into History, better than* Herodotus *and* Ctesias *and* Hellanicus, *and all that have wrote of* India. The *Satyrist* therefore had reason to say,

-----Et quicquid Graecia mendax   Audet in Historia.[D]

[A: ***Strabo Geograph.*** lib. 11. p.m. 350.]

[B: ***Strabo ibid.*** lib. 2. p.m. 48.]

[C: ***Strabo ibid.*** lib. 1 p.m. 29.]

[D: ***Juvenal. Satyr.*** X. ***vers.*** 174.]

Aristotle,[A] 'tis true, tells us, [Greek: Holos de ta men agria agriotera en tae Asia, andreiotera de panta ta en taei Europaei, polymorphotata de ta en taei libyaei;

kai legetai de tis paroimia, hoti aei pherei ti libyae kainon;] i.e. *That generally the Beasts are wilder in* Asia, *stronger in* Europe, *and of greater variety of shapes in* Africa; *for as the* Proverb *saith*, Africa *always produces something new*. *Pliny*[B] indeed ascribes it to the Heat of the *Climate, Animalium, Hominumque effigies monstriferas, circa extremitates ejus gigni, minime mirum, artifici ad forman-da Corpora, effigiesque caelandas mobilitate ignea*. But *Nature* never formed a whole *Species* of *Monsters*; and 'tis not the *heat* of the Country, but the warm and fertile Imagination of these *Historians*, that has been more productive of them, than *Africa* it self; as will farther appear by what I shall produce out of them, and particularly from the Relation that *Ctesias* makes of the *Pygmies*.

[A: *Aristotle Hist. Animal*, lib. 8. cap. 28.]

[B: *Plin. Nat. Hist.* lib. 6. cap. 30. p.m. 741.]

I am the more willing to instance in *Ctesias*, because he tells his Story roundly; he no ways minces it; his Invention is strong and fruitful; and that you may not in the least mistrust him, he pawns his word, that all that he writes, is certainly true: And so successful he has been, how Romantick soever his Stories may appear, that they have been handed down to us by a great many other Authors, and of Note too; tho' some at the same time have looked upon them as mere Fables. So that for the present, till I am better informed, and I am not over curious in it, I shall make *Ctesias*, and the other *Indian Historians*, the *Inventors* of the extravagant Relations we at present have of the *Pygmies*, and not old *Homer*. He calls them, 'tis true, from something of Resemblance of their shape, [Greek: andres]: But these *Historians* make them to speak the *Indian Language*; to use the same *Laws*; and to be so considerable a Nation, and so valiant, as that the *King* of *India* makes choice of them for his *Corps de Guards*; which utterly spoils *Homer's Simile*, in making them so little, as only to fight *Cranes*.

Ctesias's Account therefore of the *Pygmies* (as I find it in *Photius's Bibliotheca*,[A] and at the latter end of some Editions of *Herodotus*) is this:

[A: *Photij. Bibliothec. Cod.* 72. p.m. 145.]

[Greek: Hoti en mesae tae Indikae anthropoi eisi melanes, kai kalountai pygmaioi, tois allois homoglossoi Indois. mikroi de eisi lian; hoi makrotatoi auton pae-

cheon duo, hoi de pleistoi, henos haemiseos paecheos, komaen de echousi makro-
tataen, mechri kai hepi ta gonata, kai eti katoteron, kai pogona megiston panton
anthropon; epeidan oun ton pogona mega physosin, ouketi amphiennyntai ouden
emation: alla tas trichas, tas men ek taes kephalaes, opisthen kathientai poly kato
ton gonaton; tas de ek tou po gonos, emprosthen mechri podon elkomenas. Hepeita
peripykasamenoi tas trichas peri apan to soma, zonnyntai, chromenoi autais anti
himatiou, aidoion de mega echousin, hoste psauein ton sphyron auton, kai pachy.
autoite simoi te kai aischroi. ta de probata auton, hos andres. kai hai boes kai hoi
onoi, schedon hoson krioi? kai hoi hippoi auton kai hoi aemionoi, kai ta alla panta
zoa, ouden maezo krion; hepontai de toi basilei ton Indon, touton ton pygmaion
andres trischilioi. sphodra gar eisi toxotai; dikaiotatoi de eisi kai nomoisi chrontai
osper kai hoi Indoi. Dagoous te kai alopekas thaereuousin, ou tois kysin, alla koraxi
kai iktisi kai koronais kai aetois.]

Narrat praeter ista, in media India homines reperiri nigros, qui Pygmaei
appellentur. Eadem hos, qua Inda reliqui, lingua uti, sed valde esse parvos, ut
maximi duorum cubitorum, & plerique unius duntaxat cubiti cum dimidio al-
titudinem non excedant. Comam alere longissimam, ad ipsa usque genua demis-
sam, atque etiam infra, cum barba longiore, quam, apud ullos hominum. Quae
quidem ubi illis promissior esse caeperit, nulla deinceps veste uti: sed capillos
multo infra genua a tergo demissos, barbamque praeter pectus ad pedes usque
defluentem, per totum corpus in orbem constipare & cingere, atque ita pilos
ipsis suos vestimenti loco esse. Veretrum illis esse crassum ac longum, quod ad
ipsos quoque pedum malleolos pertingat. Pygmeos hosce simis esse naribus, &
deformes. Ipsorum item oves agnorem nostrotum instar esse; boves & asinos, ari-
etum fere magnitudine, equos item multosque & caetera jumenta omnia nihilo
esse nostris arietibus majora. Tria horum Pygmaeorum millia Indorum regem
in suo comitatu habere, quod sagittarij sint peritissimi. Summos esse justitiae
cultores iisdemque quibus Indi reliqui, legibus parere. Venari quoque lepores
vulpesque, non canibus, sed corvis, milvis, cornicibus, aquilis adhibitis.

In the middle of **India** (saith **Ctesias**) there are black Men, they are call'd **Pyg-**
mies, using the same Language, as the other **Indians**; they are very little, the tallest
of them being but two Cubits, and most of them but a Cubit and a half high. They

have very long hair, reaching down to their Knees and lower; and a Beard larger than any Man's. After their Beards are grown long, they wear no Cloaths, but the Hair of their Head falls behind a great deal below their Hams; and that of their Beards before comes down to their Feet: then laying their Hair thick all about their Body, they afterwards gird themselves, making use of their Hair for Cloaths. They have a *Penis* so long, that it reaches to the Ancle, and the thickness is proportionable. They are flat nosed and ill favoured. Their Sheep are like Lambs; and their Oxen and Asses scarce as big as Rams; and their Horses and Mules, and all their other Cattle not bigger. Three thousand Men of these *Pygmies* do attend the *King* of *India*. They are good *Archers*; they are very just, and use the same *Laws* as the *Indians* do. They kill Hares and Foxes, not with Dogs, but with Ravens, Kites, Crows, and Eagles.'

Well, if they are so good Sports-men, as to kill Hares and Foxes with Ravens, Kites, Crows and Eagles, I can't see how I can bring off *Homer*, for making them fight the *Cranes* themselves. Why did they not fly their *Eagles* against them? these would make greater Slaughter and Execution, without hazarding themselves. The only excuse I have is, that *Homer*'s *Pygmies* were real *Apes* like *Men*; but those of *Ctesias* were neither *Men* nor *Pygmies*; only a Creature begot in his own Brain, and to be found no where else.

Ctesias was Physician to *Artaxerxes Mnemon* as *Diodorus Siculus*[A] and *Strabo*[B] inform us. He was contemporary with *Xenophon*, a little later than *Herodotus*; and *Helvicus* in his *Chronology* places him three hundred eighty three years before *Christ*: He is an ancient Author, 'tis true, and it may be upon that score valued by some. We are beholden to him, not only for his Improvements on the Story of the *Pygmies*, but for his Remarks likewise on several other parts of *Natural History*; which for the most part are all of the same stamp, very wonderful and incredible; as his *Mantichora*, his *Gryphins*, the *horrible Indian Worm*, a Fountain of *Liquid Gold*, a Fountain of *Honey*, a Fountain whose Water will make a Man confess all that ever he did, a Root he calls [Greek: paraebon], that will attract Lambs and Birds, as the Loadstone does filings of Steel; and a great many other Wonders he tells us: all of which are copied from him by *AElian, Pliny, Solinus, Mela, Philostratus*, and others. And *Photius* concludes *Ctesias*'s Account of *India* with this passage; [Greek: Tauta graphon kai mythologon Ktaesias. legei t' alaethestata graphein; epagon hos ta men autos idon graphei, ta de par auton mathon ton eidoton. polla de touton kai alla thaumasiotera paralipein, dia to mae doxai tois mae tauta theasamenois apista syngraphein;] i.e. *These things* (saith he) Ctesias *writes and feigns, but he himself says all he has wrote is very true. Adding, that some things which he describes, he had seen himself; and the others he had learn'd from those that had seen them: That he had omitted a great many other things more wonderful, because he would not seem to those that have not seen them, to write incredibilities.* But notwithstanding all this, *Lucian*[C] will not believe a word he saith; for he tells us that *Ctesias* has wrote of *India*, [Greek: A maete autos eide, maete allou eipontos aekousen], *What he neither saw himself, nor ever heard from any Body else.* And *Aristotle* tells us plainly, he is not fit to be believed: [Greek: En de taei Indikaei hos phaesi Ktaesias, ouk on axiopistos.][D] And the same opinion *A. Gellius*[E] seems to have of him, as he had likewise of several other old *Greek Historians* which happened to fall into his hands at *Brundusium*, in his return from *Greece* into *Italy*; he gives this Character of them and their performance: *Erant autem isti omnes libri Graeci, miraculorum fabularumque pleni: res inauditae, incredulae, Scriptores veteres non parvae authoritatis*, Aristeas Proconnesius, & Isagonus, & Nicaeensis, & Ctesias, & Onesicritus, & Polystephanus, & Hegesias. Not that I think all that *Ctesias* has wrote is fabulous; For tho' I cannot believe his *speaking Pygmies*, yet what he writes of the *Bird* he calls [Greek: Bittakos], that it would speak *Greek* and the *Indian Language*, no doubt is very true; and as *H. Stephens*[F] observes in his Apology for *Ctesias*, such a Relation would seem very surprising to one, that had never seen nor heard of a *Parrot*.

[A: *Diodor. Siculi Bibliothec*. lib. 2. p.m. 118.]
[B: *Strabo Geograph*. lib. 14. p. 451.]
[C: *Lucian* lib 1. *verae Histor*. p.m. 373.]
[D: *Arist. Hist. Animal.* lib. 8. cap. 28.]
[E: *A. Gellij. Noctes. Attic.* lib. 9. cap. 4.]
[F: *Henr. Stephani de Ctesia Historico antiquissimo disquisitio, ad finem*

Herodoti.]

But this Story of **Ctesias**'s **speaking Pygmies**, seems to be confirm'd by the Account that **Nonnosus**, the Emperour **Justinian**'s Ambassador into **AEthiopia**, gives of his Travels. I will transcribe the Passage, as I find it in **Photius**,[A] and 'tis as follows:

[A: **Photij. Bibliothec.** cod. 3. p.m. 7.]

[Greek: Hoti apo taes pharsan pleonti toi Nonnosoi, epi taen eschataen ton naeson kataentaekoti toion de ti synebae, thauma kai akousai. enetuche gar tisi morphaen men kai idean echousin anthropinaen, brachytatois de to megethos, kai melasi taen chroan. hypo de trichon dedasysmenois dia pantos tou somatos. heiponto de tois andrasi kai gynaikes paraplaesiai kai paidaria eti brachytera, ton par autois andron. gymnoi de aesan hapantes; plaen dermati tini mikroi taen aido periekalypron, hoi probebaekotes homoios andres te kai gynaikes. agrion de ouden eped eiknynto oude anaemeron; alla kai phonaen eichon men anthropinaen, agnoston de pantapasi taen dialekton tois te perioikois hapasi, kai polloi pleon tois peri taen Nonnoson, diezon de ek thalattion ostreion, kai ichthyon, ton apo taes thalassaes eis taen naeson aporrhiptomenon; tharsos de eichon ouden. alla kai horontes tous kath' haemas anthropous hypeptaesan, hosper haemeis ta meiso ton thaerion.]

Naviganti a Pharsa Nonoso, & ad extremam usque insularum delato, tale quid occurrit, vel ipso auditu admirandum. Incidit enim in quosdam forma quidem & figura humana, sed brevissimos, & cutem nigros, totumque pilosos corpus. Sequebantur viros aequales foeminae, & pueri adhuc breviores. Nudi omnes agunt, pelle tantum brevi adultiores verenda tecti, viri pariter ac foeminae: agreste nihil, neque efferum quid prae se ferentes. Quin & vox illis humana, sed omnibus, etiam accolis, prorsus ignota lingua, multoque amplius Nonosi sociis. Vivunt marinis ostreis, & piscibus e mari ad insulam projectis. Audaces minime sunt, ut nostris conspectis hominibus, quemadmodum nos visa ingenti fera, metu perculsi fuerint.

'That **Nonnosus** sailing from **Pharsa**, when he came to the farthermost of the Islands, a thing, very strange to be heard of, happened to him; for he lighted on some (**Animals**) in shape and appearance like **Men**, but little of stature, and of a black colour, and thick covered with hair all over their Bodies. The Women, who were of the same stature, followed the Men: They were all naked, only the Elder of them, both Men and Women, covered their Privy Parts with a small Skin. They seemed not at all fierce or wild; they had a Humane Voice, but their *Dialect* was altogether unknown to every Body that lived about them; much more to those that were with *Nonnosus*. They liv'd upon Sea Oysters, and Fish that were cast out of the Sea, upon the Island. They had no Courage; for seeing our Men, they were frighted, as we are at the sight of the greatest wild Beast.'

[Greek: *phonaen eichon men anthropinaen*] I render here, *they had a Humane Voice*, not *Speech*: for had they spoke any Language, tho' their *Dialect* might be somewhat different, yet no doubt but some of the Neighbourhood would have understood something of it, and not have been such utter Strangers to it. Now 'twas observed of the *Orang-Outang*, that it's *Voice* was like the Humane, and it would make a Noise like a Child, but never was observed to speak, tho' it had the *Organs* of *Speech* exactly formed as they are in *Man*; and no Account that ever has been given of this Animal do's pretend that ever it did. I should rather agree to what *Pliny*[A] mentions, *Quibusdam pro Sermone nutus motusque Membrorum est*; and that they had no more a Speech than *Ctesias* his *Cynocephali* which could only bark, as the same *Pliny*[B] remarks; where he saith, *In multis autem Montibus Genus Hominum Capitibus Caninis, ferarum pellibus velari, pro voce latratum edere, unguibus armatum venatu & Aucupio vesci, horum supra Centum viginti Millia fuisse prodente se Ctesias scribit.* But in *Photius* I find, that *Ctesias's Cynocephali* did speak the *Indian Language* as well as the *Pygmies*. Those therefore in *Nonnosus* since they did not speak the *Indian*, I doubt, spoke no *Language* at all; or at least, no more than other *Brutes* do.

[A: *Plinij Nat. Hist.* lib. 6. cap. 30. p.m. 741.]

[B: *Plinij. Nat. Hist.* lib. 7. cap. 2. p.m. 11.]

Ctesias I find is the only Author that ever understood what Language 'twas that the *Pygmies* spake: For *Herodotus*[A] owns that they use a sort of Tongue like to no other, but screech like *Bats*. He saith, [Greek: Hoi Garamantes outoi tous troglodytas Aithiopas thaereuousi toisi tetrippoisi. Hoi gar Troglodytai aithiopes podas tachistoi anthropon panton eisi, ton hymeis peri logous apopheromenous akouomen. Siteontai de hoi Troglodytai ophis, kai Saurous, kai ta toiauta ton Herpeton. Glossan de oudemiaei allaei paromoiaen nenomikasi, alla tetrygasi kathaper hai nukterides;] i.e. *These* Garamantes *hunt the* Troglodyte AEthiopians *in Chariots with four Horses. The* Troglodyte AEthiopians *are the swiftest of foot of all Men that ever he heard of by any Report. The* Troglodytes *eat Serpents and Lizards, and such sort of Reptiles. They use a Language like to no other Tongue, but screech like Bats.*

[A: *Herodot. in Melpomene.* pag. 283.]

Now that the *Pygmies* are *Troglodytes*, or do live in Caves, is plain from *Aristotle*,[A] who saith, [Greek: Troglodytai de' eisi ton bion]. And so *Philostratus*,[B] [Greek: Tous de pygmaious oikein men hypogeious]. And methinks *Le Compte*'s Relation concerning the *wild* or *savage Man* in *Borneo*, agrees so well with this, that I shall transcribe it: for he tells us,[C] *That in* Borneo *this* wild *or* savage Man *is indued with extraordinary strength; and not withstanding he walks but upon two Legs, yet he is so swift of foot, that they have much ado to outrun him. People of Quality course him, as we do Stags here: and this sort of hunting is the King's usual divertisement.* And *Gassendus* in the Life of *Peiresky*, tells us they commonly hunt them too in *Angola* in *Africa*, as I have already mentioned. So that very likely *Herodotus's Troglodyte AEthiopians* may be no other than our *Orang-Outang* or *wild Man*. And the rather, because I fancy their Language is much the same: for an *Ape* will chatter, and make a noise like a *Bat*, as his *Troglodytes* did: And they undergo to this day the same Fate of being hunted, as formerly the *Troglodytes* used to be by the *Garamantes*.

[A: *Arist. Hist. Animal.*, lib. 8. cap. 15. p.m. 913.]

[B: *Philostrat. in vita Appollon. Tyanaei*, lib. 3. cap. 14. p.m. 152.]

[C: *Lewis le Compte* Memoirs and Observations on *China*, p.m. 510.]

Whether those [Greek: andras mikrous metrion elassonas andron] which the *Nasamones* met with (as *Herodotus*[A] relates) in their Travels to discover *Libya*, were the *Pygmies*; I will not determine: It seems that *Nasamones* neither understood their Language, nor they that of the *Nasamones*. However, they were so kind to the *Nasamones* as to be their Guides along the Lakes, and afterwards brought them to a City, [Greek: en taei pantas einai toisi agousi to megethos isous, chroma de melanas], i.e. *in which all were of the same stature with the Guides, and black*. Now since they were all *little black Men*, and their Language could not be understood, I do suspect they may be a Colony of the *Pygmies*: And that they were no farther Guides to the *Nasamones*, than that being frighted at the sight of them, they ran home, and the *Nasamones* followed them.

[A: *Herodotus in Euterpe* seu lib. 2. p.m. 102.]

I do not find therefore any good Authority, unless you will reckon *Ctesias* as such, that the *Pygmies* ever used a Language or Speech, any more than other *Brutes* of the same *Species* do among themselves, and that we know nothing of, whatever *Democritus* and *Melampodes* in *Pliny*,[A] or *Apollonius Tyanaeus* in *Porphyry*[B] might formerly have done. Had the *Pygmies* ever spoke any *Language* intelligible by Mankind, this might have furnished our *Historians* with notable Subjects for their *Novels*; and no doubt but we should have had plenty of them.

[A: *Plinij Nat. Hist.* lib. 10. cap. 49.]

[B: *Porphyrius de Abstinentia*, lib. 3. pag. m. 103.]

But *Albertus Magnus*, who was so lucky as to guess that the *Pygmies* were a sort of *Apes*; that he should afterwards make these *Apes* to *speak*, was very unfortunate, and spoiled all; and he do's it, methinks, so very awkwardly, that it is as difficult almost to understand his Language as his *Apes*; if the Reader has a mind to attempt it, he will find it in the Margin.[A]

[A: *Si qui Homines sunt Silvestres, sicut Pygmeus, non secundum unam rationem nobiscum dicti sunt Homines, sed aliquod habent Hominis in quadam deliberatione & Loquela, &c.* A little after adds, Voces quaedam (sc. Animalia) formant ad diversos conceptus quos habent, sicut Homo & Pygmaeus; & quaedam non faciunt hoc, sicut multitudo fere tota aliorum Animalium. Adhuc autem eorum quae ex ratione cogitativa formant voces, quaedam sunt succumbentia, quaedam autem non succumbentia. Dico autem succumbentia, a conceptu Animae cadentia & mota ad Naturae Instinctum, sicut Pygmeus, qui non, sequitur rationem Loquelae sed Naturae Instinctum; Homo autem non succumbit sed sequitur rationem. Albert. Magn. de Animal. lib. 1. cap. 3. p.m. 3.]

Had *Albertus* only asserted, that the *Pygmies* were a sort of *Apes*, his Opinion possibly might have obtained with less difficulty, unless he could have produced some Body that had heard them talk. But *Ulysses Aldrovandus*[A] is so far from believing his *Ape Pygmies* ever spoke, that he utterly denies, that there were ever any such Creatures in being, as the *Pygmies*, at all; or that they ever fought the *Cranes*. *Cum itaque Pygmaeos* (saith he) *dari negemus, Grues etiam cum iis Bellum gerere, ut fabulantur, negabimus, & tam pertinaciter id negabimus, ut ne jurantibus credemus.*

[A: *Ulys. Aldrovandi Ornitholog.* lib. 20. p.m. 344.]

I find a great many very Learned Men are of this Opinion: And in the first place, *Strabo*[A] is very positive; [Greek: Heorakos men gar oudeis exaegeitai ton pisteos axion andron;] i.e. *No Man worthy of belief did ever see them*. And upon all occasions he declares the same. So *Julius Caesar Scaliger*[B] makes them to be only a Fiction of the Ancients, *At haec omnia* (saith he) *Antiquorum figmenta & merae Nugae, si exstarent, reperirentur. At cum universus Orbis nunc nobis cognitus sit, nullibi haec Naturae Excrementa reperiri certissimum est.* And *Isaac Casaubon*[C] ridicules such as pretend to justifie them: *Sic nostra aetate* (saith he) *non desunt, qui eandem de Pygmaeis lepidam fabellam renovent; ut qui etiam e Sacris Literis, si Deo placet, fidem illis conentur astruere. Legi etiam Bergei cujusdam Galli Scripta, qui se vidisse diceret. At non ego credulus illi, illi inquam Omnium Bipedum mendacissimo.* I shall add one Authority more, and that is of *Adrian Spigelius,* who produces a Witness that had examined the very place, where the *Pygmies* were said to be; yet upon a diligent enquiry, he could neither find them, nor hear any tidings of them.[D] *Spigelius* therefore tells us, Hoc loco de Pygmaeis dicendum erat, qui [Greek: para pygonos] dicti a statura, quae ulnam non excedunt. Verum ego Poetarum fabulas esse crediderim, pro quibus tamen *Aristoteles* minime haberi vult, sed veram esse Historiam. *8. Hist. Animal. 12.* asseverat. Ego quo minus hoc statuam, tum Authoritate primum Doctissimi *Strabonis I. Geograph.* coactus sum, tum potissimum nunc moveor, quod nostro tempore, quo nulla Mundi pars est, quam Nautarum Industria non perlustrarit, nihil tamen, unquam simile aut visum est, aut auditum. Accedit quod *Franciscus Alvarez* Lusitanus, qui ea ipsa loca peragravit, circa quae Aristoteles Pygmaeos esse scribit, nullibi tamen tam parvam Gentem a se conspectam tradidit, sed Populum esse Mediocris staturae, & *AEthiopes* tradit.

[A: *Strabo Geograph.* lib. 17. p.m. 565.]

[B: *Jul. Caes. Scaliger. Comment. in Arist. Hist. Animal.* lib. 8. sec. 126. p.m. 914.]

[C: *Isaac Causabon Notae & Castigat. in* lib. 1. *Strabonis Geograph.* p.m. 38.]

[D: *Adrian. Spigelij de Corporis Humani fabrica*, lib. 1. cap. 7. p.m. 15.]

I think my self therefore here obliged to make out, that there were such Creatures as *Pygmies*, before I determine what they were, since the very being of them is called in question, and utterly denied by so great Men, and by others too that might be here produced. Now in the doing this, *Aristotle*'s Assertion of them is so very positive, that I think there needs not a greater or better Proof; and it is so remarkable a one, that I find the very Enemies to this Opinion at a loss, how to shift it off. To lessen it's Authority they have interpolated the *Text*, by foisting into the *Translation* what is not in the Original; or by not translating at all the most material passage, that makes against them; or by miserably glossing it, to make him speak what he never intended: Such unfair dealings plainly argue, that at any rate they are willing to get rid of a Proof, that otherwise they can neither deny, or answer.

Aristotle's Text is this, which I shall give with *Theodorus Gaza's* Translation: for discoursing of the Migration of Birds, according to the Season of the Year, from one Country to another, he saith:[A]

[A: *Aristotel. Hist. Animal.* lib. 8. cap. 12.]

[Greek: Meta men taen phthinoporinaen Isaemerian, ek tou Pontou kaiton psychron pheugonta ton epionta cheimona; meta de taen earinaen, ek ton therinon, eis tous topous tous psychrous, phoboumena ta kaumata; ta men, kai ek ton engus topon poioumena tas metabolas, ta de, kai ek ton eschaton hos eipein, hoion hai geranoi poiousi. Metaballousi gar ek ton Skythikon eis ta helae ta ano taes Aigyptou, othen ho Neilos rhei. Esti de ho topos outos peri on hoi pigmaioi katoikousin; ou gar esti touto mythos, all' esti kata taen alaetheian. Genos mikron men, hosper legetai, kai autoi kai hoi hippoi; Troglodytai d' eisi ton bion.]

Tam ab Autumnali AEquinoctio ex Ponto, Locisque frigidis fugiunt Hyemem futuram. A Verno autem ex tepida Regione ad frigidam sese conferunt, aestus metu futuri: & alia de locis vicinis discedunt, alia de ultimis, prope dixerim, ut Grues faciunt, quae ex Scythicis Campis ad Paludes AEgypto superiores, unde Nilus profluit, veniunt, quo in loco pugnare cum Pygmaeis dicuntur. Non enim id fabula est, sed certe, genus tum hominum, tum etiam Equorum pusillum (ut dicitur) est, deguntque in Cavernis, unde Nomen Troglodytae a subeundis Cavernis accepere.

In English 'tis thus: 'At the ***Autumnal AEquinox*** they go out of ***Pontus*** and the cold Countreys to avoid the Winter that is coming on. At the ***Vernal AEquinox*** they pass from hot Countreys into cold ones, for fear of the ensuing heat; some making their Migrations from nearer places; others from the most remote (as I may say) as the ***Cranes*** do: for they come out of ***Scythia*** to the Lakes above ***AEgypt***, whence the ***Nile*** do's flow. This is the place, whereabout the ***Pygmies*** dwell: For this is no ***Fable***, but a ***Truth***. Both they and the Horses, as 'tis said, are a small kind. They are ***Troglodytes***, or live in Caves.'

We may here observe how positive the ***Philosopher*** is, that there are ***Pygmies***; he tells us where they dwell, and that 'tis no Fable, but a Truth. But ***Theodorus Gaza*** has been unjust in translating him, by foisting in, ***Quo in loco pugnare cum Pygmaeis dicuntur***, whereas there is nothing in the Text that warrants it: As likewise, where he expresses the little Stature of the ***Pygmies*** and the Horses, there ***Gaza*** has rendered it, ***Sed certe Genus tum Hominum, tum etiam Equorum pusillum***. ***Aristotle*** only saith, [Greek: Genos mikron men hosper legetai, kai autoi, kai hoi hippoi]. He neither makes his ***Pygmies Men***, nor saith any thing of their fighting the ***Cranes***; tho' here he had a fair occasion, discoursing of the Migration of the ***Cranes*** out of ***Scythia*** to the ***Lakes*** above ***AEgypt***, where he tells us the ***Pygmies*** are. Cardan[A] therefore must certainly be out in his guess, that ***Aristotle*** only asserted the ***Pygmies*** out of Complement to his friend ***Homer***; for surely then he would not have forgot their fight with the ***Cranes***; upon which occasion only ***Homer*** mentions them.[B] I should rather think that ***Aristotle***, being sensible of the many Fables that had been raised on this occasion, studiously avoided the mentioning this fight, that he might not give countenance to the Extravagant Relations that had been made of it.

[A: *Cardan de Rerum varietate*, lib. 8. cap. 40. p.m. 153.]

[B: *Apparet ergo* (saith *Cardan*) Pygmaeorum Historiam esse fabulosam, quod & *Strabo* sentit & nosira aetas, cum omnia nunc ferme orbis mirabilia innotuerint, declarat. Sed quod tantum Philosophum decepit, fuit Homeri Auctoritas non apud illium levis.]

But I wonder that neither *Casaubon* nor *Duvall* in their Editions of *Aristotle*'s Works, should have taken notice of these Mistakes of *Gaza*, and corrected them. And *Gesner*, and *Aldrovandus*, and several other Learned Men, in quoting this place of *Aristotle*, do make use of this faulty Translation, which must necessarily lead them into Mistakes. *Sam. Bochartus*[A] tho' he gives *Aristotle*'s Text in Greek, and adds a new Translation of it, he leaves out indeed the *Cranes* fighting with the *Pygmies*, yet makes them *Men*, which *Aristotle* do's not; and by anti-placing, *ut aiunt*, he renders *Aristotle*'s Assertion more dubious; *Neque enim* (saith he in the Translation) *id est fabula, sed revera, ut aiunt, Genus ibi parvum est tam Hominum quam Equorum. Julius Caesar Scaliger* in translating this Text of *Aristotle*, omits both these Interpretations of *Gaza*; but on the other hand is no less to be blamed in not translating at all the most remarkable passage, and where the Philosopher seems to be so much in earnest; as, [Greek: ou gar esti touto mythos, all' esti kata taen alaetheian], this he leaves wholly out, without giving us his reason for it, if he had any: And Scaliger's[B] insinuation in his Comment, viz. Negat esse fabulam de his (sc. Pygmeis) *Herodotus,* at Philosophus semper moderatus & prudens etiam addidit, [Greek: hosper legetai], is not to be allowed. Nor can I assent to Sir *Thomas Brown*'s[C] remark upon this place; *Where indeed* (saith he) Aristotle *plays the* Aristotle; *that is, the wary and evading asserter; for tho' with* non est fabula *he seems at first to confirm it, yet at last he claps in,* sicut aiunt, *and shakes the belief he placed before upon it. And therefore* Scaliger (saith he) *hath not translated the first, perhaps supposing it surreptitious, or unworthy so great an Assertor.* But had *Scaliger* known it to be surreptitious, no doubt but he would have remarked it; and then there had been some Colour for the Gloss. But 'tis unworthy to be believed of *Aristotle*, who was so wary and cautious, that he should in so short a passage, contradict himself: and after he had so positively affirmed the Truth of it, presently doubt it. His [Greek: hosper legetai] therefore must have a Reference to what follows, ***Pusillum genus, ut aiunt, ipsi atque etiam Equi***, as *Scaliger* himself translates it.

[A: ***Bocharti Hierozoic. S. de Animalib. S. Script. part. Posterior***. lib. 1. cap. 11. p.m. 76.]

[B: ***Scaliger. Comment. in Arist. Hist. Animal.*** lib. 8. p.m. 914.]

[C: Sir *Thomas Brown*'s ***Pseudodoxia***, or, ***Enquiries into Vulgar Errors***, lib. 4. cap. 11.]

I do not here find ***Aristotle*** asserting or confirming any thing of the fabulous Narrations that had been made about the ***Pygmies***. He does not say that they were [Greek: andres], or [Greek: anthropoi mikroi], or [Greek: melanes]; he only calls them [Greek: pygmaioi]. And discoursing of the ***Pygmies*** in a place, where he is only treating about ***Brutes***, 'tis reasonable to think, that he looked upon them only as such. ***This is the place where the*** Pygmies ***are; this is no fable,*** saith Aristotle, as 'tis that they are a Dwarfish Race of Men; that they speak the ***Indian*** Language; that they are excellent Archers; that they are very Just; and abundance of other Things that are fabulously reported of them; and because he thought them ***Fables***, he does not take the least notice of them, but only saith, ***This is no Fable, but a Truth, that about the Lakes of*** Nile such ***Animals***, as are called ***Pygmies***, do live. And, as if he had foreseen, that the abundance of Fables that *Ctesias* (whom he saith is not to be believed) and the ***Indian Historians*** had invented about them, would make the whole Story to appear as a Figment, and render it doubtful, whether there were ever such Creatures as ***Pygmies*** in Nature; he more zealously asserts the ***Being*** of them, and assures us, That ***this is no Fable, but a Truth.***

I shall therefore now enquire what sort of Creatures these ***Pygmies*** were; and hope so to manage the Matter, as in a great measure, to abate the Passion these Great Men have had against them: for, no doubt, what has incensed them the most, was, the fabulous ***Historians*** making them a part of ***Mankind***, and then inventing a hundred ridiculous Stories about them, which they would impose upon the World as real Truths. If therefore they have Satisfaction given them in these two Points, I do not see, but that the Business may be accommodated very fairly; and that they may be allowed to be ***Pygmies***, tho' we do not make them ***Men***.

For I am not of *Gesner*'s mind, *Sed veterum nullus* (saith he[A]) *aliter de Pygmaeis scripsit, quam Homunciones esse*. Had they been a Race of *Men*, no doubt but *Aristotle* would have informed himself farther about them. Such a Curiosity could not but have excited his Inquisitive *Genius*, to a stricter Enquiry and Examination; and we might easily have expected from him a larger Account of them. But finding them, it may be, a sort of *Apes*, he only tells us, that in such a place these *Pygmies* live.

[A: *Gesner. Histor. Quadruped.* p.m. 885.]

Herodotus[A] plainly makes them *Brutes*: For reckoning up the *Animals* of *Libya*, he tells us, [Greek: Kai gar hoi ophies hoi hypermegathees, kai hoi leontes kata toutous eisi, kai hoi elephantes te kai arktoi, kai aspides te kai onoi hoi ta kerata echontes; kai hoi kynokephaloi (akephaloi) hoi en toisi staethesi tous ophthalmous echontes (hos dae legetai ge hypo libyon) kai agrioi andres, kai gynaikes agriai kai alla plaethei polla thaeria akatapseusta;] i.e. *That there are here prodigious large Serpents, and Lions, and Elephants, and Bears, and Asps, and Asses that have horns, and Cynocephali,* (in the Margin 'tis *Acephali*) that have Eyes in their Breast, (as is reported by the Libyans) and wild Men, and wild Women, and a great many other wild Beasts that are not fabulous. *Tis evident therefore that* Herodotus his [Greek: agrioi andres, kai gynaikes agriai] are only [Greek: thaeria] or wild Beasts: and tho' they are called [Greek: andres], they are no more *Men* than our *Orang-Outang*, or *Homo Sylvestris*, or *wild Man*, which has exactly the same Name, and I must confess I can't but think is the same Animal: and that the same Name has been continued down to us, from his Time, and it may be from *Homer's*.

[A: *Herodot. Melpomene seu* lib. 4. p.m. 285.]

So *Philostratus* speaking of *AEthiopia* and *AEgypt*, tells us,[A] [Greek: Boskousi de kai thaeria hoia ouch heterothi; kai anthropous melanas, ho mae allai aepeiroi. Pygmaion te en autais ethnae kai hylaktounton allo allaei.] i.e. *Here are bred wild Beasts that are not in other places; and black Men, which no other Country affords: and amongst them is the Nation of the Pygmies, and the* BARK-ERS, that is, the *Cynocephali.* For tho' *Philostratus* is pleased here only to call them *Barkers*, and to reckon them, as he does the *Black Men* and the *Pygmies* amongst the *wild Beasts* of those Countreys; yet *Ctesias*, from whom *Philostratus* has borrowed a great deal of his *Natural History*, stiles them *Men*, and makes them speak, and to perform most notable Feats in Merchandising. But not being in a merry Humour it may be now, before he was aware, he speaks Truth: For *Caelius Rhodiginus's*[B] Character of him is, *Philostratus omnium qui unquam Historiam conscripserunt, mendacissimus.*

[A: *Philostratus in vita Apollon. Tyanaei*, lib. 6. cap. 1. p.m. 258.]

[B: *Caelij Rhodigini Lection. Antiq.* lib. 17. cap. 13.]

Since the *Pygmies* therefore are some of the *Brute Beasts* that naturally breed in these Countries, and they are pleased to let us know as much, I can easily excuse them a Name. [Greek: Andres agrioi], or *Orang-Outang*, is alike to me; and I am better pleased with *Homer*'s [Greek: andres pygmaioi], than if he had called [Greek: pithaekoi]. Had this been the only Instance where they had misapplied the Name of *Man*, methinks I could be so good natur'd, as in some measure to make an Apology for them. But finding them, so extravagantly loose, so wretchedly whimsical, in abusing the Dignity of Mankind, by giving the name of *Man* to such monstrous Productions of their idle Imaginations, as the *Indian Historians* have done, I do not wonder that wise Men have suspected all that comes out of their Mint, to be false and counterfeit.

Such are their [Greek: Amykteres] or [Greek: Arrines], that want Noses, and have only two holes above their Mouth; they eat all things, but they must be raw; they are short lived; the upper part of their Mouths is very prominent. The [Greek: Enotokeitai], whose Ears reach down to their Heels, on which they lye and sleep. The [Greek: Astomoi], that have no Mouths, a civil sort of People, that dwell about the Head of the *Ganges*; and live upon smelling to boil'd Meats and the Odours of Fruits and Flowers; they can bear no ill scent, and therefore can't live in a Camp. The [Greek: Monommatoi] or [Greek: Monophthalmoi], that have but one Eye, and that in the middle of their Foreheads: they have Dog's Ears; their Hair stands an end, but smooth on the Breasts. The [Greek: Sternophthalmoi], that have Eyes in their Breasts. The [Greek: Panai sphaenokephaloi] with Heads like Wedges. The [Greek: Makrokephaloi], with great Heads. The [Greek: hyperboreoi], who live a Thousand years. The [Greek: okypodes], so swift that they will out-run a Horse. The [Greek:

opiothodaktyloi], that go with their Heels forward, and their Toes backwards. The [Greek: Makroskeleis], The [Greek: Steganopodes], The [Greek: Monoskeleis], who have one Leg, but will jump a great way, and are call'd *Sciapodes*, because when they lye on their Backs, with this *Leg* they can keep off the Sun from their Bodies.

Now *Strabo*[A] from whom I have collected the Description of these Monstrous sorts of *Men*, and they are mentioned too by *Pliny, Solinus, Mela, Philostratus*, and others; and *Munster* in his *Cosmography*[B] has given a *figure* of some of them; *Strabo*, I say, who was an Enemy to all such fabulous Relations, no doubt was prejudiced likewise against the *Pygmies*, because these *Historians* had made them a Puny Race of *Men*, and invented so many Romances about them. I can no ways therefore blame him for denying, that there were ever any such *Men Pygmies*; and do readily agree with him, that no *Man* ever saw them: and am so far from dissenting from those Great Men, who have denied them on this account, that I think they have all the reason in the World on their side. And to shew how ready I am to close with them in this Point, I will here examine the contrary Opinion, and what Reasons they give for the supporting it: For there have been some *Moderns*, as well as the *Ancients*, that have maintained that these *Pygmies* were real *Men*. And this they pretend to prove, both from *Humane Authority* and *Divine*.

[A: *Strabo Geograph.* lib. 15. p.m. 489. & lib. 2. p. 48. *& alibi.*]

[B: *Munster Cosmograph.* lib. 6. p. 1151.]

Now by *Men Pygmies* we are by no means to understand *Dwarfs*. In all Countries, and in all Ages, there has been now and then observed such *Miniture* of Mankind, or under-sized Men. *Cardan*[A] tells us he saw one carried about in a Parrot's Cage, that was but a Cubit high. *Nicephorus*[B] tells us, that in *Theodosius* the Emperour's time, there was one in *AEgypt* that was no bigger than a Partridge; yet what was to be admired, he was very Prudent, had a sweet clear Voice, and a generous Mind; and lived Twenty Years. So likewise a King of *Portugal* sent to a Duke of *Savoy*, when he married his Daughter to him, an *AEthiopian Dwarf* but three Palms high.[C] And *Thevenot*[D] tells us of the Present made by the King of the *Abyssins*, to the *Grand Seignior*, of several *little black Slaves* out of *Nubia*, and the Countries near *AEthiopia*, which being made *Eunuchs*, were to guard the Ladies of the *Seraglio*. And a great many such like Relations there are. But these being only *Dwarfs*, they must not be esteemed the *Pygmies* we are enquiring about, which are represented as a *Nation*, and the whole Race of them to be of the like stature. *Dari tamen integras Pumilionum Gentes, tam falsum est, quam quod falsissimum*, saith *Harduin*.[E]

[A: *Cardan de subtilitate*, lib. 11. p. 458.]

[B: *Nicephor. Histor. Ecclesiiast.* lib. 12. cap. 37.]

[C: *Happelius in Relat. curiosis*, No. 85. p. 677.]

[D: *Thevenot. Voyage de Levant.* lib. 2. c. 68.]

[E: *Jo. Harduini Notae in Plinij Nat. Hist.* lib. 6. cap. 22. p. 688.]

Neither likewise must it be granted, that tho' in some *Climates* there might be *Men* generally of less stature, than what are to be met with in other Countries, that they are presently *Pygmies*. *Nature* has not fixed the same standard to the growth of *Mankind* in all Places alike, no more than to *Brutes* or *Plants*. The Dimensions of them all, according to the *Climate*, may differ. If we consult the Original, *viz. Homer* that first mentioned the *Pygmies*, there are only these two *Characteristics* he gives of them. That they are [Greek: Pygmaioi] *seu Cubitales*; and that the *Cranes* did use to fight them. 'Tis true, as a *Poet*, he calls them [Greek: andres], which I have accounted for before. Now if there cannot be found such *Men* as are *Cubitales*, that the *Cranes* might probably fight with, notwithstanding all the Romances of the *Indian Historians*, I cannot think these *Pygmies* to be *Men*, but they must be some other *Animals*, or the whole must be a Fiction.

Having premised this, we will now enquire into their Assertion that maintain the *Pygmies* to be a Race of *Men*. Now because there have been *Giants* formerly, that have so much exceeded the usual Stature of *Man*, that there must be likewise *Pygmies* as defective in the other extream from this Standard, I think is no conclusive Argument, tho' made use of by some. Old *Caspar Bartholine*[A] tells us, that because *J. Cassanius* and others had wrote *de Gygantibus*, since no Body else had undertaken it, he would give us a Book *de Pygmaeis*; and since he makes it his design to prove the Existence of *Pygmies*, and that the *Pygmies* were *Men*, I must confess I expected great Matters from him.

[A: ***Caspar. Bartholin. Opusculum de Pygmaeis.***]

But I do not find he has informed us of any thing more of them, than what ***Jo. Talentonius***, a Professor formerly at ***Parma***, had told us before in his ***Variarum & Reconditarum Rerum Thesaurus***,[A] from whom he has borrowed most of this ***Tract***. He has made it a little more formal indeed, by dividing it into ***Chapters***; of which I will give you the ***Titles***; and as I see occasion, some Remarks thereon: They will not be many, because I have prevented my self already. The ***first Chapter*** is, ***De Homuncionibus & Pumilionilus seu Nanis a Pygmaeis distinctis***. The ***second Chapter, De Pygmaei nominibus & Etymologia***. The ***third Chapter, Duplex esse Pygmaeorum Genus; & primum Genus aliquando dari***. He means ***Dwarfs***, that are no ***Pygmies*** at all. The ***fourth Chapter*** is, ***Alterum Genus, nempe Gentem Pygmaeorum esse, aut saltem aliquando fuisse Autoritatibus Humanis, fide tamen dignorum asseritur***. 'Tis as I find it printed; and no doubt an Error in the printing. The Authorities he gives, are, ***Homer, Ctesias, Aristotle, Philostratus, Pliny, Juvenal, Oppian, Baptista Mantuan***, St. ***Austin*** and his ***Scholiast. Ludovic. Vives, Jo. Laurentius Anania, Joh. Cassanius, Joh. Talentonius, Gellius, Pomp. Mela***, and ***Olaus Magnus***. I have taken notice of most of them already, as I shall of St. ***Austin*** and ***Ludovicus Vives*** by and by. ***Jo. Laurentius Anania***[B] ex Mercatorum relatione tradit (saith ***Bartholine***) eos (sc. Pygmaeos) in Septentrionali Thraciae Parte reperiri, (quae Scythiae est proxima) atque ibi cum Gruibus pugnare. ***And*** Joh. Cassanius[C] (as he is here quoted) saith, ***De Pygmaeis fabulosa quidem esse omnia, quae de iis narrari solent, aliquando existimavi. Verum cum videam non unum vel alterum, sed complures Classicos & probatos Autores de his Homunculis multa in eandem fere Sententiam tradidisse; eo adducor ut Pygmaeos fuisse inficiari non ausim.*** He next brings in ***Jo. Talentonius***, to whom he is so much beholden, and quotes his Opinion, which is full and home, ***Constare arbitror*** (saith ***Talentonius***)[D] ***debere concedi, Pygmaeos non solum olim fuisse, sed nunc etiam esse, & homines esse, nec parvitatem illis impedimenta esse quo minus sint & homines sint.*** But were there such ***Men Pygmies*** now in being, no doubt but we must have heard of them; some or other of our Saylors, in their Voyages, would have lighted on them. Tho' ***Aristotle*** is here quoted, yet he does not make them *Men*; So neither does *Anania*: And I must own, tho' *Talentonius* be of this Opinion, yet he takes notice of the faulty Translation of this Text of *Aristotle* by *Gaza*: and tho' the parvity or lowness of Stature, be no Impediment, because we have frequently seen such *Dwarf-Men*, yet we did never see a *Nation* of them: For then there would be no need of that *Talmudical* Precept which *Job. Ludolphus*[E] mentions, *Nanus ne ducat Nanam, ne forte oriatur ex iis Digitalis* (in *Bechor.* fol. 45).

[A: *Jo. Talentionij. Variar. & Recondit. Rerum. Thesaurus.* lib. 3. cap. 21.]

[B: *Joh. Laurent. Anania prope finem tractatus primi suae Geograph.*]

[C: *Joh. Cassanius libello de Gygantibus*, p. 73.]

[D: *Jo. Talentonius Variar. & recondit. Rerum Thesaurus*, lib. 3. cap. 21. p.m. 515.]

[E: *Job Ludolphi Comment. in Historiam AEthiopic.* p.m. 71.]

I had almost forgotten *Olaus Magnus*, whom *Bartholine* mentions in the close of this Chapter, but lays no great stress upon his Authority, because he tells us, he is fabulous in a great many other Relations, and he writes but by hear-say, that the *Greenlanders* fight the *Cranes*; *Tandem* (saith *Bartholine*) *neque ideo Pygmaei sunt, si forte sagittis & hastis, sicut alij homines, Grues conficiunt & occidunt.* This I think is great Partiality: For *Ctesias*, an Author whom upon all turns *Bartholine* makes use of as an Evidence, is very positive, that the *Pygmies* were excellent *Archers*: so that he himself owns, that their being such, illustrates very much that *Text* in *Ezekiel*, on which he spends good part of the next *Chapter*, whose Title is, *Pygmaeorum Gens ex Ezekiele, atque rationibus probabilibus adstruitur*; which we will consider by and by. And tho' *Olaus Magnus* may write some things by hear-say, yet he cannot be so fabulous as *Ctesias*, who (as *Lucian* tells us) writes what he neither saw himself, or heard from any Body else. Not that I think *Olaus Magnus* his *Greenlanders* were real *Pygmies*, no more than *Ctesias* his *Pygmies* were real *Men*; tho' he vouches very notably for them. And if all that have copied this Fable from *Ctesias*, must be look'd upon as the same Evidence with himself; the number of the *Testimonies* produced need not much concern us, since they must all stand or fall with him.

The *probable Reasons* that *Bartholine* gives in the *fifth Chapter*, are taken from other *Animals*, as Sheep, Oxen, Horses, Dogs, the *Indian Formica* and Plants: For observing in the same *Species* some excessive large, and others extreamly little, he infers, Quae certe cum in Animalibus & Vegetabilibus fiant; cur in Humana specie non sit probabile, haud video: imprimis cum detur magnitudinis excessus Gigantaeus; cur non etiam dabitur Defectus? Quia ergo dantur Gigantes, dabuntur & Pygmaei. Quam consequentiam ut firmam, admittit Cardanus,[A] licet de Pygmaeis hoc tantum concedat, qui pro miraculo, non pro Gente. *Now Cardan, tho' he allows this Consequence, yet in the same place he gives several Reasons why the* Pygmies *could not be* Men*, and looks upon the whole Story as fabulous.* Bartholine *concludes this* Chapter *thus:* Ulterius ut Probabilitatem fulciamus, addendum Sceleton Pygmaei, quod *Dresdae* vidimus inter alia plurima, servatum in Arce sereniss. *Electoris Saxoniae,* altitudine infra Cubitum, Ossium soliditate, proportioneque tum Capitis, tum aliorum; ut Embrionem, aut Artificiale quid Nemo rerum peritus suspicari possit. Addita insuper est Inscriptio *Veri Pygmaei. I hereupon looked into Dr.* Brown*'s Travels into those Parts, who has given us a large Catalogue of the Curiosities, the* Elector *of* Saxony *had at* Dresden*, but did not find amongst them this* Sceleton*; which, by the largeness of the Head, I suspect to be the* Sceleton *of an* Orang-Outang*, or our* wild Man. But had he given us either a figure of it, or a more particular Description, it had been a far greater Satisfaction.

[A: *Cardan. de Rerum varietate*, lib. 8. cap. 40.]

The Title of *Bartholine*'s *sixth Chapter* is, *Pygmaeos esse aut fuisse ex variis eorum adjunctis, accidentibus*, &c. *ab Authoribus descriptis ostenditur.* As first, their *Magnitude*: which he mentions from *Ctesias, Pliny, Gellius*, and *Juvenal*; and tho' they do not all agree exactly, 'tis nothing. *Autorum hic dissensus nullus est* (saith *Bartholine*) *etenim sicut in nostris hominibus, ita indubie in Pygmaeis non omnes ejusdem magnitudinis.* 2. The *Place* and *Country*: As *Ctesias* (he saith) places them in the middle of *India*; *Aristotle* and *Pliny* at the Lakes above *AEgypt*; *Homer*'s *Scholiast* in the middle of *AEgypt*; *Pliny* at another time saith they are at the Head of the *Ganges*, and sometimes at *Gerania*, which is in *Thracia*, which being near *Scythia*, confirms (he saith) *Anania's Rela-*

*tion. **Mela*** places them at the ***Arabian Gulf***; and ***Paulus Jovius docet Pygmaeos
ultra Japonem esse***; and adds, ***has Autorum dissensiones facile fuerit conciliare;
nec mirum diversas relationes a***, Plinio ***auditas.*** For (saith he) as the ***Tartars*** often change their Seats, since they do not live in Houses, but in Tents, so 'tis no wonder that the ***Pygmies*** often change theirs, since instead of Houses, they live in Caves
or Huts, built of Mud, Feathers, and Egg-shells. And this mutation of their Habitations he thinks is very plain from ***Pliny***, where speaking of ***Gerania***, he saith, ***Pygmaeorum Gens*** fuisse (non jam esse) proditur, creduntque a Gruibus fugatos.
Which passage (saith ***Bartholine***) had ***Adrian Spigelius*** considered, he would not
so soon have left ***Aristotle's*** Opinion, because ***Franc. Alvares*** the ***Portuguese*** did
not find them in the place where ***Aristotle*** left them; for the ***Cranes***, it may be, had
driven them thence. His third Article is, their ***Habitation***, which ***Aristotle*** saith
is in ***Caves***; hence they are ***Troglodytes***. ***Pliny*** tells us they build Huts with Mud,
Feathers, and Egg-shells. But what ***Bartholine*** adds, ***Eo quod Terrae Cavernas in-
habitent, non injuria dicti sunt olim Pygmaei, Terrae filii***, is wholly new to me,
and I have not met with it in any Author before: tho' he gives us here several other
significations of the word ***Terrae filij*** from a great many Authors, which I will not
trouble you at present with. 4. The ***Form***, being flat nosed and ugly, as ***Ctesias***. 5.
Their ***Speech***, which was the same as the ***Indians***, as ***Ctesias***; and for this I find he
has no other Author. 6. Their ***Hair***; where he quotes ***Ctesias*** again, that they make
use of it for ***Clothes***. 7. Their ***Vertues and Arts***; as that they use the same Laws as
the ***Indians***, are very just, excellent Archers, and that the King of ***India*** has Three
thousand of them in his Guards. All from ***Ctesias***. 8. Their ***Animals***, as in ***Ctesias***;
and here are mentioned their Sheep, Oxen, Asses, Mules, and Horses. 9. Their various ***Actions***; as what ***Ctesias*** relates of their killing Hares and Foxes with Crows,
Eagles, &c. and fighting the ***Cranes***, as ***Homer, Pliny, Juvenal***.

The ***seventh Chapter*** in ***Bartholine*** has a promising Title, ***An Pygmaei sint
homines***, and I expected here something more to our purpose; but I find he rather
endeavours to answer the Reasons of those that would make them ***Apes***, than to
lay down any of his own to prove them ***Men***. And ***Albertus Magnus's*** Opinion he
thinks absurd, that makes them part Men part Beasts; they must be either one or the

other, not a *Medium* between both; and to make out this, he gives us a large Quotation out of *Cardan*. But *Cardan*[A] in the same place argues that they are not Men. As to *Suessanus*[B] his Argument, that they want *Reason*, this he will not Grant; but if they use it less or more imperfectly than others (which yet, he saith, is not certain) by the same parity of Reason *Children*, the *Boeotians*, *Cumani* and *Naturals* may not be reckoned *Men*; and he thinks, what he has mentioned in the preceding *Chapter* out of *Ctesias*, &c. shews that they have no small use of Reason. As to *Suessanus*'s next Argument, that they want Religion, Justice, &c. this, he saith, is not confirmed by any grave Writer; and if it was, yet it would not prove that they are not *Men*. For this defect (he saith) might hence happen, because they are forced to live in *Caves* for fear of the *Cranes*; and others besides them, are herein faulty. For this Opinion, that the *Pygmies* were *Apes* and not *Men*, he quotes likewise *Benedictus Varchius*,[C] and *Joh. Tinnulus*,[D] and *Paulus Jovius*,[E] and several others of the Moderns, he tells us, are of the same mind. *Imprimis Geographici quos non puduit in Mappis Geographicis loco Pygmaeorum simias cum Gruibus pugnantes ridicule dipinxisse.*

[A: *Cardan. de Rerum varietate*, lib. 8. cap. 40.]

[B: *Suessanus Comment. in Arist. de Histor. Animal.* lib. 8. cap. 12.]

[C: *Benedict. Varchius de Monstris. lingua vernacula.*]

[D: *Joh. Tinnulus in Glotto-Chrysio.*]

[E: *Paulus Jovius lib. de Muscovit. Legalione.*]

The Title of *Bartholine's eighth* and last *Chapter* is, *Argumenta eorum qui Pygmaeorum Historiam fabulosam censent, recitantur & refutantur.* Where he tells us, the only Person amongst the Ancients that thought the Story of the *Pygmies* to be fabulous was *Strabo*; but amongst the Moderns there are several, as *Cardan, Budaeus, Aldrovandus, Fullerus* and others. The first Objection (he saith) is that of *Spigelius* and others; that since the whole World is now discovered, how happens it, that these *Pygmies* are not to be met with? He has seven Answers to this Objection; how satisfactory they are, the Reader may judge, if he pleases, by perusing them amongst the Quotations.[A] *Cardan*'s second Objection (he saith) is, that they live but eight years, whence several Inconveniences would happen, as *Cardan* shews; he answers that no good Author asserts this; and if there was, yet what *Cardan* urges would not follow; and instances out of *Artemidorus* in *Pliny*,[B] as a *Parallel* in the *Calingae* a Nation in *India, where the Women conceive when five years old, and do not live above eight.* *Gesner* speaking of the *Pygmies*, saith, *Vitae autem longitudo anni arciter octo ut* Albertus *refert.* *Cardan* perhaps had his Authority from *Albertus*, or it may be both took it from this passage in *Pliny*, which I think would better agree to *Apes* than *Men*. But *Artemidorus* being an *Indian Historian*, and in the same place telling other Romances, the less Credit is to be given to him. The third Objection, he saith, is of *Cornelius a Lapide*, who denies the *Pygmies*, because *Homer* was the first Author of them. The fourth Objection he saith is, because Authors differ about the Place where they should be: This, he tells us, he has answered already in the fifth Chapter. The *fifth* and last Objection he mentions is, that but few have seen them. He answers, there are a great many Wonders in Sacred and Profane History that we have not seen, yet must not deny. And he instances in three; As the *Formicae Indicae*, which are as big as great Dogs: The *Cornu Plantabile* in the Island *Goa*, which when cut off from the Beast, and flung upon the Ground, will take root like a *Cabbage*: and the *Scotland Geese* that grow upon Trees, for which he quotes a great many Authors, and so concludes.

[A: *Respondeo.* 1. *Contrarium testari Mercatorum Relationem apud* Ananiam *supra Cap. 4.* 2. *Et licet non inventi essent vivi a quolibet, pari jure Monocerota & alia negare liceret.* 3. *Qui maria pernavigant, vix oras paucas maritimas lustrant, adeo non terras omnes a mari dissitas.* 4. *Neque in Oris illos habitare maritimis ex Capite quinto manifestum est.* 5. *Quis testatum se omnem adhibuisse diligentiam in inquirendo eos ut inveniret.* 6. *Ita in terra habitant, ut in Antris vitam tolerare dicantur.* 7. *Si vel maxime omni ab omnibus diligentia quaesiti fuissent, nec inventi; fieri potest, ut instar Gigantum jam desierint nec sint amplius.*]

[B: *Plinij Hist. Nat.* lib. 7. cap. 2. p.m. 14.]

Now how far *Bartholine* in his Treatise has made out that the *Pygmies* of the Ancients were real *Men*, either from the Authorities he has quoted, or his Reasonings upon them, I submit to the Reader. I shall proceed now (as I promised) to consider the Proof they pretend from *Holy Writ*: For *Bartholine* and others insist upon that *Text* in *Ezekiel* (*Cap. 27. Vers. 11*) where the *Vulgar* Translation has it thus; *Filij Arvad cum Exercitu tuo supra Muros tuos per circuitum, & Pygmaei in Turribus tuis fuerunt; Scuta sua suspenderunt supra Muros tuos per circuitum.* Now *Talentonius* and *Bartholine* think that what *Ctesias* relates of the *Pygmies*, as their being good *Archers*, very well illustrates this Text of *Ezekiel*: I shall here transcribe what Sir *Thomas Brown*[A] remarks upon it; and if any one requires further Satisfaction, they may consult *Job Ludolphus's Comment* on his *AEthiopic History*.[B]

[A: Sir *Thomas Brown's Enquiries into Vulgar Errors*, lib. 4. cap. 11. p. 242.]
[B: *Comment. in Hist. AEthiopic.* p. 73.]

The *second Testimony* (saith Sir *Thomas Brown*) *is deduced from Holy Scripture; thus rendered in the Vulgar Translation*, Sed & Pygmaei qui erant in turribus tuis, pharetras suas suspenderunt in muris tuis per gyrum: *from whence notwithstanding we cannot infer this Assertion, for first the Translators accord not, and the Hebrew word* Gammadim *is very variously rendered. Though* Aquila, Vatablus *and* Lyra *will have it* Pygmaei, *yet in the* Septuagint, *it is no more than Watchman; and so in the* Arabick *and* High-Dutch. *In the* Chalde, Cappadocians, *in* Symmachus, Medes, *and in the* French, *those of* Gamed. Theodotian *of old, and* Tremillius *of late, have retained the Textuary word; and so have the* Italian, Low Dutch, *and* English *Translators, that is, the Men of* Arvad *were upon thy Walls round about, and the* Gammadims *were in thy Towers.*

Nor do Men only dissent in the Translation of the word, but in the Exposition of the Sense and Meaning thereof; for some by Gammadims *understand a People of* Syria, *so called from the City of* Gamala; *some hereby understand the* Cappadocians, *many the* Medes: *and hereof* Forerius *hath a singular Exposition, conceiving the Watchmen of* Tyre, *might well be called* Pygmies, *the Towers of that City being so high, that unto Men below, they appeared in a Cubital Stature. Others expound it quite contrary to common Acception, that is not Men of the least, but of the largest size; so doth* Cornelius *construe* Pygmaei, *or* Viri Cubitales, *that is, not Men of a Cubit high, but of the largest Stature, whose height like that of Giants, is rather to be taken by the Cubit than the Foot; in which phrase we read the measure of* Goliah, *whose height is said to be six Cubits and span. Of affinity hereto is also the Exposition of* Jerom; *not taking* Pygmies for Dwarfs, but stout and valiant Champions; not taking the sense of [Greek: pygmae], which signifies the Cubit measure, but that which expresseth Pugils; that is, Men fit for Combat and the Exercise of the Fist. Thus there can be no satisfying illation from this Text, the diversity, or rather contrariety of Expositions and Interpretations, distracting more than confirming the Truth of the Story.

But why *Aldrovandus* or *Caspar Bartholine* should bring in St. *Austin* as a Favourer of this Opinion of *Men Pygmies*, I see no Reason. To me he seems to assert quite the contrary: For proposing this Question, *An ex propagine* Adam *vel filiorum* Noe, *quaedam genera Hominum Monstrosa prodierunt?* He mentions a great many monstrous Nations of *Men*, as they are described by the *Indian Historians*, and amongst the rest, the *Pygmies*, the *Sciopodes*, &c. And adds, *Quid dicam de* Cynocephalis, *quorum Canina Capita atque ipse Latratus magis Bestias quam Homines confitentur? Sed omnia Genera Hominum, quae dicuntur esse, esse credere, non est necesse.* And afterwards so fully expresses himself in favour of the *Hypothesis* I am here maintaining, that I think it a great Confirmation of it. *Nam & Simias* (saith he) *& Cercopithecos, & Sphingas, si nesciremus non Homines esse, sed Bestias, possent isti Historici de sua Curiositate gloriantes velut Gentes Aliquas Hominum nobis impunita vanitate mentiri.* At last he concludes and determines the Question thus, *Aut illa, quae talia de quibusdam Gentibus scripta sunt, omnino nulla sunt, aut si sunt, Homines non sunt, aut ex* Adam *sunt si Homines sunt.*

There is nothing therefore in St. *Austin* that justifies the being of *Men Pygmies*, or that the *Pygmies* were *Men*; he rather makes them *Apes*. And there is nothing in his *Scholiast Ludovicus Vives* that tends this way, he only quotes from other Authors, what might illustrate the Text he is commenting upon, and no way asserts their being *Men*. I shall therefore next enquire into *Bochartus*'s Opinion, who would have them to be the *Nubae* or *Nobae. Hos Nubas Troglodyti-*

cos (saith[A] he) ***ad Avalitem Sinum esse Pygmaeos Veterum multa probant.*** He gives us five Reasons to prove this. As, 1. The Authority of ***Hesychius***, who saith, [Greek: Noboi Pygmaioi]. 2. Because ***Homer*** places the ***Pygmies*** near the Ocean, where the Nubae were. 3. ***Aristotle*** places them at the lakes of the ***Nile***. Now by the ***Nile Bochartus*** tells us, we must understand the ***Astaborus***, which the Ancients thought to be a Branch of the ***Nile***, as he proves from ***Pliny, Solinus*** and ***AEthicus***. And ***Ptolomy*** (he tells us) places the ***Nubae*** hereabout. 4. Because ***Aristotle*** makes the ***Pygmies*** to be ***Troglodytes***, and so were the ***Nubae***. 5. He urges that Story of ***Nonnosus*** which I have already mentioned, and thinks that those that ***Nonnosus*** met with, were a Colony of the ***Nubae***; but afterwards adds, ***Quos tamen absit ut putemus Statura fuisse Cubitali, prout Poetae fingunt, qui omnia in majus augent.*** But this methinks spoils them from being ***Pygmies***; several other Nations at this rate may be ***Pygmies*** as well as these ***Nubae***. Besides, he does not inform us, that these ***Nubae*** used to fight the ***Cranes***; and if they do not, and were not ***Cubitales***, they can't be ***Homer***'s ***Pygmies***, which we are enquiring after. But the Notion of their being ***Men***, had so possessed him, that it put him upon fancying they must be the ***Nubae***; but 'tis plain that those in ***Nonnosus*** could not be a Colony of the ***Nubae***; for then the ***Nubae*** must have understood their Language, which the ***Text*** saith, none of the Neighbourhood did. And because the ***Nubae*** are ***Troglodytes***, that therefore they must be ***Pygmies***, is no Argument at all. For ***Troglodytes*** here is used as an ***Adjective***; and there is a sort of ***Sparrow*** which is called ***Passer Troglodytes***. Not but that in ***Africa*** there was a Nation of ***Men*** called ***Troglodytes***, but quite different from our ***Pygmies***. How far ***Bochartus*** may be in the right, in guessing the Lakes of the ***Nile*** (whereabout ***Aristotle*** places the ***Pygmies***) to be the Fountains of the River ***Astaborus***, which in his description, and likewise the ***Map***, he places in the Country of the ***Avalitae***, near the ***Mossylon Emporium***; I shall not enquire. This I am certain of, he misrepresents ***Aristotle*** where he tells us,[B] ***Quamvis in ea fabula hoc saltem verum esse asserat Philosophus, Pusillos Homines in iis locis degere***: for as I have already observed; ***Aristotle*** in that ***Text*** saith nothing at all of their being ***Men***: the contrary rather might be thence inferred, that they were ***Brutes***. And ***Bochart's*** Translation, as well as ***Gaza's*** is faulty here, and by no means to be allowed, *viz. Ut aiunt, genus ibi parvum est tam Homi-num, quam Equorum*; which had *Bochartus* considered he would not have been so fond it may be of his *Nubae*. And if the [Greek: Noboi Pygmaioi] in *Hesychius* are such *Pygmies* as *Bochartus* makes his *Nubae, Quos tamen absit ut putemus staturta fuisse Cubitali*, it will not do our business at all; and neither *Homer's* Authority, nor *Aristotle's* does him any Service.

[A: *Sam. Bochart. Geograph. Sacrae*, Part. 1. lib. 2. cap. 23. p.m. 142.]

[B: *Bocharti Hierozoici pars Posterior*, lib. I. cap. II. p. 76.]

But this Fable of *Men Pygmies* has not only obtained amongst the *Greeks* and *Indian Historians*: the *Arabians* likewise tell much such Stories of them, as the same learned *Bochartus* informs us. I will give his Latin Translation of one of them, which he has printed in *Arabick* also: *Arabes idem* (saith[A] *Bochartus*) *referunt ex cujusdam* Graeculi *fide, qui* Jacobo Isaaci *filio*, Sigariensi *fertur ita narrasse. Navigabam aliquando in mari* Zingitano, *& impulit me ventus in quandam Insulam. In cujus Oppidum cum devenissem, reperi Incolas Cubitalis esse staturae, & plerosque Coclites. Quorum multitudo in me congregata me deduxit ad Regem suum. Fussit is, ut Captivus detinerer; & inquandam Caveae speciem conjectus sum; eos autem aliquando ad bellum instrui cum viderem, dixerunt Hostem imminere, & fore ut propediem ingrueret. Nec multo post Gruum exercitus in eos insurrexit. Atque ideo erant Coclites, quod eorum oculos hae confodissent. Atque Ego, virga assumpta, in eas impetum feci, & illae avolarunt atque aufugerunt; ob quod facinus in honore fui apud illos*. This Author, it seems, represents them under the same Misfortune with the *Poet*, who first mentioned them, as being blind, by having their Eyes peck'd out by their cruel Enemies. Such an Accident possibly might happen now and then, in these bloody Engagements, tho' I wonder the *Indian Historians* have not taken notice of it. However the *Pygmies* shewed themselves grateful to their Deliverer, in heaping *Honours* on him. One would guess, for their own sakes, they could not do less than make him their *Generalissimo*; but our Author is modest in not declaring what they were.

[A: *Bochartus ibid*. p.m. 77.]

Isaac Vossius seems to unsettle all, and endeavours utterly to ruine the whole

Story: for he tells us, If you travel all over *Africa*, you shall not meet with either a *Crane* or *Pygmie*: *Se mirari* (saith[A] *Isaac Vossius*) Aristotelem, *quod tam serio affirmet non esse fabellam, quae de Pygmaeis & Bello, quod cum Gruibus gerant, narrantur. Si quis totam pervadat* Africam, *nullas vel Grues vel Pygmaeos inveniet*. Now one would wonder more at *Vossius*, that he should assert this of *Aristotle*, which he never said. And since *Vossius* is so mistaken in what he relates of *Aristotle*; where he might so easily have been in the right, 'tis not improbable, but he may be out in the rest too: For who has travelled all *Africa* over, that could inform him? And why should he be so peremptory in the Negative, when he had so positive an Affirmation of *Aristotle* to the contrary? or if he would not believe *Aristotle's* Authority, methinks he should *Aristophanes's*, who tells us,[B] [Greek: Speirein hotau men Geranos kroizon es taen libyaen metachorae]. *'Tis time to sow when the noisy Cranes take their flight into* Libya. Which Observation is likewise made by *Hesiod, Theognis, Aratus*, and others. And *Maximus Tyrius* (as I find him quoted in *Bochartus*) saith, [Greek: Hai geravoi ex Aigyptou ora therous aphistamenai, ouk anechomenai to thalpos teinasai pterygas hosper istia, pherontai dia tou aeros euthy ton Skython gaes]. i.e. *Grues per aestatem ex* AEgypto *abscedentes, quia Calorem pati non possunt, alis velorum instar expansis, per aerem ad* Scythicam *plagam recta feruntur*. Which fully confirms that Migration of the *Cranes* that *Aristotle* mentions.

[A: *Isaac Vossius de Nili aliorumque stuminum Origine*, Cap. 18.]

[B: *Aristophanes in Nubibus*.]

But *Vossius* I find, tho' he will not allow the *Cranes*, yet upon second Thoughts did admit of *Pygmies* here: For this Story of the *Pygmies* and the *Cranes* having made so much *noise*, he thinks there may be something of truth in it; and then gives us his Conjecture, how that the *Pygmies* may be those *Dwarfs*, that are to be met with beyond the Fountains of the *Nile*; but that they do not fight *Cranes* but *Elephants*, and kill a great many of them, and drive a considerable Traffick for their teeth with the *Jagi*, who sell them to those of *Congo* and the *Portuguese*. I will give you *Vossius's* own words; *Attamen* (saith[A] he) *ut solent fabellae non de nihilo fingi & aliquod plerunque continent veri, id ipsum quoque que hic fac-*

tum esse existimo. Certum quippe est ultra Nili *fontes multos reperiri* Nanos, *qui tamen non cum Gruibus, sed cum Elephantis perpetuum gerant bellum. Prae-cipuum quippe Eboris commercium in regno magni* Macoki *per istos transigitur Homunciones; habitant in Sylvis, & mira dexteritate Elephantos sagittis confici-unt. Carnibus vescuntur, Dentes vero* Jagis *divendunt, illi autem* Congentibus & Lusitanis.

[A: *Isaac Vossius ibid.*]

Job Ludolphus[A] in his *Commentary* on his *AEthiopick History* remarks, That there was never known a Nation all of Dwarfs. *Nani quippe* (saith *Ludol-phus*) *Naturae quodam errore ex aliis justae staturae hominibus generantur. Qualis vero ea Gens sit, ex qua ista Naturae Ludibria tanta copia proveniant, Vossium docere oportelat, quia Pumiliones Pumiles alios non gignunt, sed ple-runque steriles sunt, experientia teste; ut plane non opus habuerunt Doctores Talmudici Nanorum matrimonia prohibere, ne Digitales ex iis nascerentur. Ludolphus* it may be is a little too strict with *Vossius* for calling them *Nani*; he may only mean a sort of Men in that Country of less Stature than ordinary. And *Dap-per* in his History of *Africa*, from whom *Vossius* takes this Account, describes such in the Kingdom of *Mokoko*, he calls *Mimos*, and tells us that they kill *Elephants*. But I see no reason why *Vossius* should take these Men for the *Pygmies* of the An-cients, or think that they gave any occasion or ground for the inventing this Fable, is there was no other reason, this was sufficient, because they were able to kill the *El-ephants*. The *Pygmies* were scarce a Match for the *Cranes*; and for them to have encountered an *Elephant*, were as vain an Attempt, as the *Pygmies* were guilty of in *Philostratus*[B] 'who to revenge the Death of *Antaeus*, having found *Hercu-les* napping in *Libya*, mustered up all their Forces against him. One *Phalanx* (he tells us) assaulted his left hand; but against his right hand, that being the stronger, two *Phalanges* were appointed. The Archers and Slingers besieged his feet, admir-ing the hugeness of his Thighs: But against his Head, as the Arsenal, they raised Bat-teries, the King himself taking his Post there. They set fire to his Hair, put Reaping-hooks in his Eyes; and that he might not breath, clapp'd Doors to his Mouth and Nostrils; but all the Execution that they could do, was only to awake him, which when done, deriding their folly, he gather'd them all up in his Lion's Skin, and carried them (**Philostratus** thinks) to **Euristhenes.**' This **Antaeus** was as remarkable for his height, as the **Pygmies** were for their lowness of Stature: For **Plutarch**[C] tells us, that **Q. Sterorius** not being willing to trust Common Fame, when he came to **Tingis** (now **Tangier**) he caused **Antaeus's** Sepulchre to be opened, and found his Corps full threescore Cubits long. But **Sterorius** knew well enough how to impose upon the Credulity of the People, as is evident from the Story of his **white Hind**, which **Plutarch** likewise relates.

[A: ***Job Ludolphus in Comment, in Historiam AEthiopicam***, p.m. 71.]

[B: ***Philostratus. Icon.*** lib. 2. p.m. 817.]

[C: ***Plutarch. in vita Q. Sertorij***.]

But to return to our **Pygmies**; tho' most of the great and learned Men would seem to decry this Story as a Fiction and mere Fable, yet there is something of Truth, they think, must have given the first rise to it, and that it was not wholly the product of Phancy, but had some real foundation, tho' disguised, according to the different Imagination and **Genius** of the **Relator**: 'Tis this that has incited them to give their several Conjectures about it. **Job Ludolphus** finding what has been offered at in Relation to the **Pygmies**, not to satisfie, he thinks he can better account for this Story, by leaving out the **Cranes**, and placing in their stead, another sort of Bird he calls the **Condor**. I will give you his own words: ***Sed ad Pygmaeos*** (saith [A] ***Ludolphus***) ***revertamur; fabula de Geranomachia Pygmaeorum seu pugna cum Gruibus etiam aliquid de vero trahere videtur, si pro Gruibus*** Condoras ***intelligas, Aves in interiore*** Africa ***maximas, ut fidem pene excedat; aiunt enim quod Ales ista vitulum Elephanti in Aerem extollere possit; ut infra docebimus. Cum his Pygmaeos pugnare, ne pecora sua rapiant, incredibile non est. Error ex eo natus videtur, quod primus Relator, alio vocabulo destitutus, Grues pro Condoris nominarit, sicuti*** Plautus ***Picos pro Gryphilus***, & Romani ***Boves lucas pro Elephantis dixere***.

[A: ***Job Ludolphus Comment, in Historiam suam AEthiopic.*** p. 73.]

'Tis true, if what **Juvenal** only in ridicule mentions, was to be admitted as a thing really done, that the **Cranes** could fly away with a **Pygmie**, as our **Kites** can with a Chicken, there might be some pretence for **Ludovicus's Condor** or **Cunctor**: For he mentions afterwards[A] out of **P. Joh. dos Santos** the **Portuguese**, that 'twas observed that one of these **Condors** once flew away with an Ape, Chain, Clog and all, about ten or twelve pounds weight, which he carried to a neighbouring Wood, and there devoured him. And **Garcilasso de la Vega**[B] relates that they will seize and fly away with a Child ten or twelve years old. But **Juvenal**[C] only mentions this in ridicule and merriment, where he saith,

Adsubitas Thracum volucres, nubemque sonoram   Pygmaeos parvis currit Bellator in armis: Mox impar hosti, raptusque per aera curvis Unguibus a faeva fertur Grue.

[A: **Job Ludolphus ibid**. pag. 164.]
[B: **Garcilasso de la Vega Royal Comment**, of Peru.]
[C: **Juvenal Satyr**. 13 **vers**. 167.]

Besides, were the **Condors** to be taken for the **Cranes**, it would utterly spoil the **Pygmaeomachia**; for where the Match is so very unequal, 'tis impossible for the Pygmies to make the least shew of a fight. **Ludolphus** puts as great hardships on them, to fight these **Condors**, as **Vossius** did, in making them fight **Elephants**, but not with equal Success; for **Vossius**'s **Pygmies** made great Slaughters of the Elephants; but **Ludolphus** his **Cranes** sweep away the **Pygmies**, as easily as an **Owl** would a **Mouse**, and eat them up into the bargain; now I never heard the **Cranes** were so cruel and barbarous to their Enemies, tho' there are some Nations in the World that are reported to do so.

Moreover, these **Condor**'s I find are very rare to be met with; and when they are, they often appear single or but a few. Now **Homer**'s, and the **Cranes** of the Ancients, are always represented in Flocks. Thus **Oppian**[A] as I find him translated into Latin Verse:

Et velut AEthiopum veniunt, Nilique fluenta
Turmalim Palamedis Aves, celsoeque per altum
Aera labentes fugiunt Athlanta nivosum,
Pygmaeos imbelle Genus, parvumque saligant,
Non perturbato procedunt ordine densae

Instructis volucres obscurant aera Turmis.

To imagine these *Grues* a single Gigantick Bird, would much lessen the Beauty of *Homer's Simile*, and would not have served his turn; and there are none who have borrowed Homer's fancy, but have thought so. I will only farther instance in *Baptista Mantuan*:

Pygmaei breve vulgus, iners Plelecula, quando
Convenere Grues longis in praelia rostris,
Sublato clamore fremunt, dumque agmine magno
Hostibus occurrit, tellus tremit Indica, clamant
Littora, arenarum nimbis absconditur aer;
Omnis & involvit Pulvis solemque, Polumque,
Et Genus hoc Hominum natura imbelle, quietum,
Mite, facit Mavors pugnax, immane Cruentum.

[Footnote: A *Oppian lib. I. de Piscibus*.]
Having now considered and examined the various Opinions of these learned Men concerning this *Pygmaeomachia*; and represented the Reasons they give for maintaining their Conjectures; I shall beg leave to subjoyn my own: and if what at present I offer, may seem more probable, or account for this Story with more likelyhood, than what hath hitherto been advanced, I shall not think my time altogether misspent: But if this will not do, I shall never trouble my head more about them, nor think my self any ways concerned to write on this Argument again. And I had not done it now, but upon the occasion of Dissecting this *Orang-Outang*, or *wild Man*, which being a Native of *Africa*, and brought from *Angola*, tho' first taken higher up in the Country, as I was informed by the Relation given me; and observing so great a Resemblance, both in the outward shape, and, what surprized me more, in the Structure likewise of the inward Parts, to a *Man*; this Thought was easily suggested to me, That very probably this *Animal*, or some other such of the same *Species*, might give the first rise and occasion to the Stories of the *Pygmies*. What has been the [Greek: proton pheudos], and rendered this Story so dif-

ficult to be believed, I find hath been the Opinion that has generally obtained, that these *Pygmies* were really a Race of *little Men*. And tho' they are only *Brutes*, yet being at first call'd *wild Men*, no doubt from the Resemblance they bear to *Men*; there have not been wanting those especially amongst the Ancients, who have invented a hundred ridiculous Stories concerning them; and have attributed those things to them, were they to be believed in what they say, that necessarily conclude them real *Men*.

To sum up therefore what I have already discoursed, I think I have proved, that the *Pygmies* were not an *Humane Species* or *Men*. And tho' *Homer*, who first mentioned them, calls them [Greek: andres pygmaioi], yet we need not understand by this Expression any thing more than *Apes*: And tho' his *Geranomachia* hath been look'd upon by most only as a Poetical Fiction; yet by assigning what might be the true Cause of this Quarrel between the *Cranes* and *Pygmies*, and by divesting it of the many fabulous Relations that the *Indian Historians*, and others, have loaded it with, I have endeavoured to render it a true, at least a probable Story. I have instanced in *Ctesias* and the *Indian Historians*, as the Authors and Inventors of the many Fables we have had concerning them: Particularly, I have Examined those Relations, where Speech or Language is attributed to them; and shewn, that there is no reason to believe that they ever spake any Language at all. But these *Indian Historians* having related so many extravagant Romances of the *Pygmies*, as to render their whole History suspected, nay to be utterly denied, that there were ever any such Creatures as *Pygmies* in *Nature*, both by *Strabo* of old, and most of our learned men of late, I have endeavoured to assert the Truth of their *being*, from a *Text* in *Aristotle*; which being so positive in affirming their Existence, creates a difficulty, that can no ways be got over by such as are of the contrary Opinion. This *Text* I have vindicated from the false Interpretations and Glosses of several Great Men, who had their Minds so prepossessed and prejudiced with the Notion of *Men Pygmies*, that they often would quote it, and misapply it, tho' it contain'd nothing that any ways favoured their Opinion; but the contrary rather, that they were *Brutes*, and not *Men*.

And that the *Pygmies* were really *Brutes*, I think I have plainly proved out of *Herodotus* and *Philostratus*, who reckon them amongst the *wild Beasts* that breed in those Countries: For tho' by **Herodotus** they are call'd [Greek: andres agrioi], and **Philostratus** calls them [Greek: anthropous melanas], yet both make them [Greek: theria] or **wild Beasts**. And I might here add what **Pausanias**[A] relates from **Euphemus Car**, who by contrary Winds was driven upon some Islands, where he tells us, [Greek: en de tautais oikein andras agrious], but when he comes to describe them, tells us that they had no Speech; that they had Tails on their Rumps; and were very lascivious toward the Women in the Ship. But of these more, when we come to discourse of **Satyrs**.

　　[A: **Pausanias in Atticis**, p.m. 21.]

　　And we may the less wonder to find that they call **Brutes Men**, since 'twas common for these **Historians** to give the Title of **Men**, not only to **Brutes**, but they were grown so wanton in their Inventions, as to describe several Nations of **Monstrous Men**, that had never any Being, but in their own Imagination, as I have instanced in several. I therefore excuse **Strabo**, for denying the **Pygmies**, since he could not but be convinced, they could not be such **Men**, as these **Historians** have described them. And the better to judge of the Reasons that some of the Moderns have given to prove the Being of **Men Pygmies**, I have laid down as **Postulata's**, that hereby we must not understand **Dwarfs**, nor yet a Nation of **Men**, tho' somewhat of a lesser size and stature than ordinary; but we must observe those two Characteristicks that **Homer** gives of them, that they are **Cubitales** and fight **Cranes**.

　　Having premised this, I have taken into consideration **Caspar Bartholine Senior** his **Opusculum de Pygmaeis**, and **Jo. Talentonius**'s Dissertation about them: and upon examination do find, that neither the Humane Authorities, nor Divine that they alledge, do any ways prove, as they pretend, the Being of **Men Pygmies**. St. **Austin**, who is likewise quoted on their side, is so far from favouring this Opinion, that he doubts whether any such Creatures exist, and if they do, concludes them to be **Apes** or **Monkeys**; and censures those **Indian Historians** for imposing such Beasts upon us, as distinct Races of **Men**. **Julius Caesar Scaliger**, and **Isaac Casaubon**, and **Adrian Spigelius** utterly deny the Being of **Pygmies**, and look upon them as a Figment only of the Ancients, because such little Men as they describe them to be, are no where to be met with in all the World. The Learned **Bochartus** tho' he esteems the *Geranomachia* to be a Fable, and slights it, yet thinks that what might give the occasion to the Story of the *Pygmies*, might be the *Nubae* or *Nobae*; as *Isaac Vossius* conjectures that it was those *Dwarfs* beyond the Fountains of the *Nile*, that *Dapper* calls the *Mimos*, and tells us, they kill *Elephants* for to make a Traffick with their Teeth. But *Job Ludolphus* alters the Scene, and instead of *Cranes*, substitutes his *Condors*, who do not fight the *Pygmies*, but fly away with them, and then devour them.

Now all these Conjectures do no ways account for *Homer's Pygmies* and *Cranes*, they are too much forced and strain'd. Truth is always easie and plain. In our present Case therefore I think the *Orang-Outang*, or *wild Man*, may exactly supply the place of the *Pygmies*, and without any violence or injury to the Story, sufficiently account for the whole History of the *Pygmies*, but what is most apparently fabulous; for what has been the greatest difficulty to be solved or satisfied, was their being *Men*; for as *Gesner* remarks (as I have already quoted him) *Sed veterum nullus aliter de Pygmaeis scripsit, quam Homunciones esse*. And the Moderns too, being byassed and misguided by this Notion, have either wholly denied them, or contented themselves in offering their Conjectures what might give the first rise to the inventing this Fable. And tho' *Albertus*, as I find him frequently quoted, thought that the *Pygmies* might be only a sort of *Apes*, and he is placed in the Head of those that espoused this Opinion, yet he spoils all, by his way of reasoning, and by making them speak; which was more than he needed to do.

I cannot see therefore any thing that will so fairly solve this doubt, that will reconcile all, that will so easily and plainly make out this Story, as by making the *Orang-Outang* to be the *Pygmie* of the Ancients; for 'tis the same Name that Antiquity gave them. For *Herodotus*'s [Greek: andres agrioi], what can they be else, than *Homines Sylvestres*, or *wild Men*? as they are now called. And *Homer*'s [Greek: andres pygmaioi], are no more an Humane Kind, or Men, then *Herodotus*'s [Greek: andres agrioi], which he makes to be [Greek: theria], or *wild Beasts*: And the [Greek: andres mikroi] or [Greek: melanes] (as they are often called) were just the same. Because this sort of *Apes* had so great a resemblance to Men, more than other *Apes* or *Monkeys*; and they going naturally erect, and being designed by Nature to go so, (as I have shewn in the *Anatomy*) the Ancients had a very plausible ground for giving them this denomination of [Greek: andres] or [Greek: anthropoi], but commonly they added an Epithet; as [Greek: agrioi, mikroi, pygmaioi, melanes], or some such like. Now the Ancient **Greek** and **Indian Historians**, tho' they might know these **Pygmies** to be only **Apes** like **Men**, and not to be real **Men**, yet being so extremely addicted to **Mythology**, or making Fables, and finding this so fit a Subject to engraft upon, and invent Stories about, they have not been wanting in furnishing us with a great many very Romantick ones on this occasion. And the Moderns being imposed upon by them, and misguided by the Name of [Greek: andres] or [Greek: anthropoi], as if thereby must be always understood an **Humane Kind**, or **real Men**, they have altogether mistaken the Truth of the Story, and have either wholly denied it, or rendered it as improbable by their own Conjectures.

This difficulty therefore of their being called **Men**, I think, may fairly enough be accounted by what I have said. But it may be objected that the **Orang-Outang**, or these **wild** or **savage Men** are not [Greek: pygmaioi], or **Trispithami**, that is, but two Foot and a quarter high, because by some Relations that have been given, it appears they have been observed to be of a higher stature, and as tall as ordinary Men. Now tho' this may be allowed as to these **wild Men** that are bred in other places; and probably enough like wise, there are such in some Parts of the Continent of **Africa**; yet 'tis sufficient to our business if there are any there, that will come within our Dimensions; for our Scene lies in **Africa**; where **Strabo** observes, that generally the Beasts are of a less size than ordinary; and this he thinks might give rise to the Story of the **Pygmies**. For, saith he[A] [Greek: Ta de boskaemata autois esti mikra, probata kai aiges, kai kynes mikroi, tracheis de kai machimoi (oikountes mikroi ontes) tacha de kai tous pygmaious apo tes touton mikrophyias epenoaesan, kai aneplasan.] i.e. *That their Beasts are small, as their Sheep, Goats and Oxen, and their Dogs are small, but hairy and fierce: and it may be* (saith he) from the [Greek: mikrophyia] or littleness of the stature of these Animals, they have invented and imposed on us the **Pygmies. And then adds,** That no body fit to be believed ever saw them; *because he fancied, as a great many others have done, that these* Pygmies *must be* real Men, *and not a sort of* Brutes. *Now since the other* Brutes *in this Country are generally of a less size than in other Parts, why may not this sort of* Ape, *the* Orang-Outang, *or* wild Man, *be so likewise.* Aristotle *speaking of the* Pygmies, saith, [Greek: genos mikron men kai autoi, kai oi hippoi.] *That both they and the Horses there are but small.* He does not say *their* Horses, for they were never mounted upon *Horses*, but only upon *Partridges, Goats* and *Rams*. And as the *Horses*, and other *Beasts* are naturally less in *Africa* than in other Parts, so likewise may the *Orang-Outang* be. This that I dissected, which was brought from *Angola* (as I have often mentioned) wanted something of the just stature of the *Pygmies*; but it was young, and I am therefore uncertain to what tallness it might grow, when at full Age: And neither *Tulpius*, nor *Gassendus*, nor any that I have hitherto met with, have adjusted the full stature of this *Animal* that is found in those parts from whence ours was brought: But 'tis most certain, that there are sorts of *Apes* that are much less than the *Pygmies* are described to be. And, as other *Brutes*, so the *Ape-kind*, in different Climates, may be of different Dimensions; and because the other *Brutes* here are generally small, why may not *they* be so likewise. Or if the difference should be but little, I see no great reason in this case, why we should be over-nice, or scrupulous.

[A: *Strabo Geograph*. lib. 17. p.m. 565.]

As to our *Ape Pygmies* or *Orang-Outang* fighting the *Cranes*, this, I think, may be easily enough made out, by what I have already observed; for this *wild Man* I dissected was Carnivorous, and it may be Omnivorous, at least as much as *Man* is; for it would eat any thing that was brought to the Table. And if it was not their Hunger that drove them to it, their Wantonness, it may be, would make them apt enough to rob the *Cranes* Nests; and if they did so, no doubt but the *Cranes* would noise enough about it, and endeavour what they could to beat them off, which a Poet might easily make a Fight: Tho' *Homer* only makes use of it as a *Simile*, in comparing the great Shouts of the *Trojans* to the Noise of the *Cranes*, and the Silence of the *Greeks* to that of the *Pygmies* when they are going to Engage, which is natural enough, and very just, and contains nothing, but what may easily be believed; tho' upon this account he is commonly exposed, and derided, as the Inventor of this Fable; and that there was nothing of Truth in it, but that 'twas wholly a Fiction of his own.

Those *Pygmies* that *Paulus Jovius*[A] describes, tho' they dwell at a great distance from *Africa*, and he calls them *Men*, yet are so like *Apes*, that I cannot think them any thing else. I will give you his own words: ***Ultra Lapones*** (saith he) ***in Regione inter Corum & Aquilonem perpetua oppressa Caligine*** Pygmaeos ***reperiri, aliqui eximiae fidei testes retulerunt; qui postquam ad summum adoleverint, nostratis Pueri denum annorum Mensuram vix excedunt. Meticulosum genus hominum, & garritu Sermonem exprimens, adeo ut tam Simiae propinqui, quam Statura ac sensibus ab justae Proceritatis homine remoti videantur***. Now there is this Advantage in our *Hypothesis*, it will take in all the *Pygmies*, in any part of the World; or wherever they are to be met with, without supposing, as some have done, that 'twas the *Cranes* that forced them to quit their Quarters; and upon this account several Authors have described them in different places: For unless we suppose the *Cranes* so kind to them, as to waft them over, how came we to find them often in Islands? But this is more than can be reasonably expected from so great Enemies.

[A: ***Paul. Jovij de Legatione Muschovitar***. lib. p.m. 489.]

I shall conclude by observing to you, that this having been the Common Error of the Age, in believing the *Pygmies* to be a sort of *little Men*, and it having been handed down from so great Antiquity, what might contribute farther to the confirming of this Mistake, might be, the Imposture of the Navigators, who failing to Parts where these *Apes* are, they have embalmed their Bodies, and brought them home, and then made the People believe that they were the *Men* of those Countries from whence they came. This *M.P. Venetus* assures us to have been done; and 'tis not unlikely: For, saith he,[A] ***Abundat quoque Regio ipsa*** (sc. Basman in Java majori) ***diversis Simiis magnis & parvis, hominibus simillimis, hos capiunt Venatores & totos depilant, nisi quod, in barba & in loco secreto Pilos relinquunt, & occisos speciebus Aromaticis condiunt, & postea desiccant, venduntque Negociatoribus, qui per diversas Orbis Partes Corpora illa deferentes, homines persuadent Tales Homunciones in Maris Insulis reperiri. Joh. Jonston***[B] relates the same thing, but without quoting the Author; and as he is very apt to do, commits a great mistake, in telling us, ***pro Homunculis marinis venditant***.

[A: ***M. Pauli Veneti de Regionibus Oriental***. lib. 3. cap. 15. p. m. 390.]

[B: *Jo. Jonston. Hist. Nat. de Quadruped*. p.m. 139.]

I shall only add, That the Servile Offices that these Creatures are observed to perform, might formerly, as it does to this very day, impose upon Mankind to believe, that they were of the same *Species* with themselves; but that only out of Sullenness or cunning, they think they will not *speak*, for fear of being made Slaves. *Philostratus*[A] tells us, That the *Indians* make use of the *Apes* in gathering the Pepper; and for this Reason they do defend and preserve them from the *Lions*, who are very greedy of preying upon them: And altho' he calls them *Apes*, yet he speaks of them as *Men*, and as if they were the Husbandmen of the *Pepper Trees*, [Greek: kai ta dendra oi piperides, on georgoi pithekoi]. And he calls them the People of *Apes*; [Greek: ou legetai pithekon oikein demos en mychois tou orous]. *Dapper*[B] tells us, *That the Indians take the* Baris *when young, and make them so tame, that they will do almost the work of a Slave; for they commonly go erect as Men do. They will beat Rice in a Mortar, carry Water in a Pitcher*, &c. And Gassendus[C] in the Life of *Pieresky*, tells us, us, *That they will play upon a Pipe or Cittern, or the like Musick, they will sweep the House, turn the Spit, beat in a Mortar, and do other Offices in a Family*. And *Acosta*, as I find him quoted by *Garcilasso de la Vega*[D] tells us of a *Monkey* he saw at the Governour's House at *Cartagena*, 'whom they fent often to the Tavern for Wine, with Money in one hand, and a Bottle in the other; and that when he came to the Tavern, he would not deliver his Money, until he had received his Wine. If the Boys met with him by the way, or made a houting or noise after him, he would set down his Bottle, and throw Stones at them; and having cleared the way he would take up his Bottle, and hasten home, And tho' he loved Wine excessively, yet he would not dare to touch it, unless his Master gave him License.' A great many Instances of this Nature might be given that are very surprising. And in another place he tells us, That the Natives think that they can speak, but will not, for fear of being made to work. And *Bontius*[E] mentions that the *Javans* had the same Opinion concerning the *Orang-Outang*, *Loqui vero eos, easque Javani aiunt, sed non velle, ne ad labores cogerentur*.

[A: *Philostratus in vita Apollonij Tyanaei*, lib. 3. cap. I. p. m. 110, & 111.]

[B: *Dapper Description de l'Afrique*, p.m. 249.]

[C: *Gassendus in vita Pierskij*, lib. 5. p.m. 169.]

[D: *Garcilasso de la Vega Royal Commentaries of Peru*, lib. 8. cap. 18. p. 1333.]

[E: *Jac. Bontij Hist. Nat. & Med*. lib. 5. cap. 32. p.m. 85.]

The Codes Of Hammurabi And Moses
W. W. Davies

QTY

The discovery of the Hammurabi Code is one of the greatest achievements of archaeology, and is of paramount interest, not only to the student of the Bible, but also to all those interested in ancient history...

Religion   **ISBN: *1-59462-338-4***   **Pages:132**

MSRP $12.95

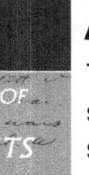

The Theory of Moral Sentiments
Adam Smith

QTY

This work from 1749. contains original theories of conscience amd moral judgment and it is the foundation for systemof morals.

Philosophy   **ISBN: *1-59462-777-0***   **Pages:536**

MSRP $19.95

Jessica's First Prayer
Hesba Stretton

QTY

In a screened and secluded corner of one of the many railway-bridges which span the streets of London there could be seen a few years ago, from five o'clock every morning until half past eight, a tidily set-out coffee-stall, consisting of a trestle and board, upon which stood two large tin cans, with a small fire of charcoal burning under each so as to keep the coffee boiling during the early hours of the morning when the work-people were thronging into the city on their way to their daily toil...

Pages:84

Childrens   **ISBN: *1-59462-373-2***   *MSRP $9.95*

My Life and Work
Henry Ford

QTY

Henry Ford revolutionized the world with his implementation of mass production for the Model T automobile. Gain valuable business insight into his life and work with his own auto-biography... "We have only started on our development of our country we have not as yet, with all our talk of wonderful progress, done more than scratch the surface. The progress has been wonderful enough but..."

Pages:300

Biographies/   **ISBN: *1-59462-198-5***   *MSRP $21.95*

The Art of Cross-Examination
Francis Wellman

QTY

I presume it is the experience of every author, after his first book is published upon an important subject, to be almost overwhelmed with a wealth of ideas and illustrations which could readily have been included in his book, and which to his own mind, at least, seem to make a second edition inevitable. Such certainly was the case with me; and when the first edition had reached its sixth impression in five months, I rejoiced to learn that it seemed to my publishers that the book had met with a sufficiently favorable reception to justify a second and considerably enlarged edition. ..

Pages:412

Reference   **ISBN:** *1-59462-647-2*   *MSRP $19.95*

On the Duty of Civil Disobedience
Henry David Thoreau

QTY

Thoreau wrote his famous essay, On the Duty of Civil Disobedience, as a protest against an unjust but popular war and the immoral but popular institution of slave-owning. He did more than write—he declined to pay his taxes, and was hauled off to gaol in consequence. Who can say how much this refusal of his hastened the end of the war and of slavery ?

Law   **ISBN:** *1-59462-747-9*   **Pages:48**

MSRP $7.45

Dream Psychology Psychoanalysis for Beginners
Sigmund Freud

QTY

Sigmund Freud, born Sigismund Schlomo Freud (May 6, 1856 - September 23, 1939), was a Jewish-Austrian neurologist and psychiatrist who co-founded the psychoanalytic school of psychology. Freud is best known for his theories of the unconscious mind, especially involving the mechanism of repression; his redefinition of sexual desire as mobile and directed towards a wide variety of objects; and his therapeutic techniques, especially his understanding of transference in the therapeutic relationship and the presumed value of dreams as sources of insight into unconscious desires.

Pages:196

Psychology   **ISBN:** *1-59462-905-6*   *MSRP $15.45*

The Miracle of Right Thought
Orison Swett Marden

QTY

Believe with all of your heart that you will do what you were made to do. When the mind has once formed the habit of holding cheerful, happy, prosperous pictures, it will not be easy to form the opposite habit. It does not matter how improbable or how far away this realization may see, or how dark the prospects may be, if we visualize them as best we can, as vividly as possible, hold tenaciously to them and vigorously struggle to attain them, they will gradually become actualized, realized in the life. But a desire, a longing without endeavor, a yearning abandoned or held indifferently will vanish without realization.

Pages:360

Self Help   **ISBN:** *1-59462-644-8*   *MSRP $25.45*

QTY

☐ **The Rosicrucian Cosmo-Conception Mystic Christianity** *by Max Heindel* ISBN: *1-59462-188-8* **$38.95**
The Rosicrucian Cosmo-conception is not dogmatic, neither does it appeal to any other authority than the reason of the student. It is: not controversial, but is: sent forth in the, hope that it may help to clear.. New Age/Religion Pages 646

☐ **Abandonment To Divine Providence** *by Jean-Pierre de Caussade* ISBN: *1-59462-228-0* **$25.95**
"The Rev. Jean Pierre de Caussade was one of the most remarkable spiritual writers of the Society of Jesus in France in the 18th Century. His death took place at Toulouse in 1751. His works have gone through many editions and have been republished... Inspirational/Religion Pages 400

☐ **Mental Chemistry** *by Charles Haanel* ISBN: *1-59462-192-6* **$23.95**
Mental Chemistry allows the change of material conditions by combining and appropriately utilizing the power of the mind. Much like applied chemistry creates something new and unique out of careful combinations of chemicals the mastery of mental chemistry... New Age Pages 354

☐ **The Letters of Robert Browning and Elizabeth Barret Barrett 1845-1846 vol II** ISBN: *1-59462-193-4* **$35.95**
by Robert Browning and Elizabeth Barrett Biographies Pages 596

☐ **Gleanings In Genesis (volume I)** *by Arthur W. Pink* ISBN: *1-59462-130-6* **$27.45**
Appropriately has Genesis been termed "the seed plot of the Bible" for in it we have, in germ form, almost all of the great doctrines which are afterwards fully developed in the books of Scripture which follow... Religion/Inspirational Pages 420

☐ **The Master Key** *by L. W. de Laurence* ISBN: *1-59462-001-6* **$30.95**
In no branch of human knowledge has there been a more lively increase of the spirit of research during the past few years than in the study of Psychology, Concentration and Mental Discipline. The requests for authentic lessons in Thought Control, Mental Discipline and... New Age/Business Pages 422

☐ **The Lesser Key Of Solomon Goetia** *by L. W. de Laurence* ISBN: *1-59462-092-X* **$9.95**
This translation of the first book of the "Lemegton" which is now for the first time made accessible to students of Talismanic Magic was done, after careful collation and edition, from numerous Ancient Manuscripts in Hebrew, Latin, and French... New Age/Occult Pages 92

☐ **Rubaiyat Of Omar Khayyam** *by Edward Fitzgerald* ISBN:*1-59462-332-5* **$13.95**
Edward Fitzgerald, whom the world has already learned, in spite of his own efforts to remain within the shadow of anonymity, to look upon as one of the rarest poets of the century, was born at Bredfield, in Suffolk, on the 31st of March, 1809. He was the third son of John Purcell... Music Pages 172

☐ **Ancient Law** *by Henry Maine* ISBN: *1-59462-128-4* **$29.95**
The chief object of the following pages is to indicate some of the earliest ideas of mankind, as they are reflected in Ancient Law, and to point out the relation of those ideas to modern thought. Religion/History Pages 452

☐ **Far-Away Stories** *by William J. Locke* ISBN: *1-59462-129-2* **$19.45**
"Good wine needs no bush, but a collection of mixed vintages does. And this book is just such a collection. Some of the stories I do not want to remain buried for ever in the museum files of dead magazine-numbers an author's not unpardonable vanity..." Fiction Pages 272

☐ **Life of David Crockett** *by David Crockett* ISBN: *1-59462-250-7* **$27.45**
"Colonel David Crockett was one of the most remarkable men of the times in which he lived. Born in humble life, but gifted with a strong will, an indomitable courage, and unremitting perseverance... Biographies/New Age Pages 424

☐ **Lip-Reading** *by Edward Nitchie* ISBN: *1-59462-206-X* **$25.95**
Edward B. Nitchie, founder of the New York School for the Hard of Hearing, now the Nitchie School of Lip-Reading, Inc, wrote "LIP-READING Principles and Practice". The development and perfecting of this meritorious work on lip-reading was an undertaking... How-to Pages 400

☐ **A Handbook of Suggestive Therapeutics, Applied Hypnotism, Psychic Science** ISBN: *1-59462-214-0* **$24.95**
by Henry Munro Health/New Age/Health/Self-help Pages 376

☐ **A Doll's House: and Two Other Plays** *by Henrik Ibsen* ISBN: *1-59462-112-8* **$19.95**
Henrik Ibsen created this classic when in revolutionary 1848 Rome. Introducing some striking concepts in playwriting for the realist genre, this play has been studied the world over. Fiction/Classics/Plays 308

☐ **The Light of Asia** *by sir Edwin Arnold* ISBN: *1-59462-204-3* **$13.95**
In this poetic masterpiece, Edwin Arnold describes the life and teachings of Buddha. The man who was to become known as Buddha to the world was born as Prince Gautama of India but he rejected the worldly riches and abandoned the reigns of power when... Religion/History/Biographies Pages 170

☐ **The Complete Works of Guy de Maupassant** *by Guy de Maupassant* ISBN: *1-59462-157-8* **$16.95**
"For days and days, nights and nights, I had dreamed of that first kiss which was to consecrate our engagement, and I knew not on what spot I should put my lips..." Fiction/Classics Pages 240

☐ **The Art of Cross-Examination** *by Francis L. Wellman* ISBN: *1-59462-309-0* **$26.95**
Written by a renowned trial lawyer, Wellman imparts his experience and uses case studies to explain how to use psychology to extract desired information through questioning. How-to/Science/Reference Pages 408

☐ **Answered or Unanswered?** *by Louisa Vaughan* ISBN: *1-59462-248-5* **$10.95**
Miracles of Faith in China Religion Pages 112

☐ **The Edinburgh Lectures on Mental Science (1909)** *by Thomas* ISBN: *1-59462-008-3* **$11.95**
This book contains the substance of a course of lectures recently given by the writer in the Queen Street Hall, Edinburgh. Its purpose is to indicate the Natural Principles governing the relation between Mental Action and Material Conditions... New Age/Psychology Pages 148

☐ **Ayesha** *by H. Rider Haggard* ISBN: *1-59462-301-5* **$24.95**
Verily and indeed it is the unexpected that happens! Probably if there was one person upon the earth from whom the Editor of this, and of a certain previous history, did not expect to hear again... Classics Pages 380

☐ **Ayala's Angel** *by Anthony Trollope* ISBN: *1-59462-352-X* **$29.95**
The two girls were both pretty, but Lucy who was twenty-one who supposed to be simple and comparatively unattractive, whereas Ayala was credited, as her Bombwhat romantic name might show, with poetic charm and a taste for romance. Ayala when her father died was nineteen... Fiction Pages 484

☐ **The American Commonwealth** *by James Bryce* ISBN: *1-59462-286-8* **$34.45**
An interpretation of American democratic political theory. It examines political mechanics and society from the perspective of Scotsman James Bryce Politics Pages 572

☐ **Stories of the Pilgrims** *by Margaret P. Pumphrey* ISBN: *1-59462-116-0* **$17.95**
This book explores pilgrims religious oppression in England as well as their escape to Holland and eventual crossing to America on the Mayflower, and their early days in New England... History Pages 268

QTY

The Fasting Cure *by Sinclair Upton*   ISBN: *1-59462-222-1*   **$13.95**
In the Cosmopolitan Magazine for May, 1910, and in the Contemporary Review (London) for April, 1910, I published an article dealing with my experi-
ences in fasting. I have written a great many magazine articles, but never one which attracted so much attention... New Age/Self Help/Health Pages 164

Hebrew Astrology *by Sepharial*   ISBN: *1-59462-308-2*   **$13.45**
In these days of advanced thinking it is a matter of common observation that we have left many of the old landmarks behind and that we are now pressing
forward to greater heights and to a wider horizon than that which represented the mind-content of our progenitors...   Astrology Pages 144

Thought Vibration or The Law of Attraction in the Thought World   ISBN: *1-59462-127-6*   **$12.95**
by William Walker Atkinson   *Psychology/Religion Pages 144*

Optimism *by Helen Keller*   ISBN: *1-59462-108-X*   **$15.95**
Helen Keller was blind, deaf, and mute since 19 months old, yet famously learned how to overcome these handicaps, communicate with the world, and
spread her lectures promoting optimism. An inspiring read for everyone...   Biographies/Inspirational Pages 84

Sara Crewe *by Frances Burnett*   ISBN: *1-59462-360-0*   **$9.45**
In the first place, Miss Minchin lived in London. Her home was a large, dull, tall one, in a large, dull square, where all the houses were alike, and all the
sparrows were alike, and where all the door-knockers made the same heavy sound...   Childrens/Classic Pages 88

The Autobiography of Benjamin Franklin *by Benjamin Franklin*   ISBN: *1-59462-135-7*   **$24.95**
The Autobiography of Benjamin Franklin has probably been more extensively read than any other American historical work, and no other book of its kind
has had such ups and downs of fortune. Franklin lived for many years in England, where he was agent...   Biographies/History Pages 332

Name	
Email	
Telephone	
Address	
City, State ZIP	

☐ **Credit Card**   ☐ **Check / Money Order**

Credit Card Number	
Expiration Date	
Signature	

Please Mail to: *Book Jungle*
PO Box 2226
Champaign, IL 61825
or Fax to: *630-214-0564*

ORDERING INFORMATION

web*: www.bookjungle.com*
email*: sales@bookjungle.com*
fax*: 630-214-0564*
mail*: Book Jungle PO Box 2226 Champaign, IL 61825*
or PayPal *to sales@bookjungle.com*

Please contact us for bulk discounts

DIRECT-ORDER TERMS

**20% Discount if You Order
Two or More Books**
Free Domestic Shipping!
Accepted: Master Card, Visa,
Discover, American Express

www.ingramcontent.com/pod-product-compliance
Lightning Source LLC
Chambersburg PA
CBHW082014170626
46817CB00009B/3094